*What use is a kiss within a marriage of convenience?*

It was a brief and unremarkable ceremony, each of them pledging to honor and obey the other, followed by the minister pronouncing them man and wife.

Maura noticed the preacher's perplexed look when Luther didn't take advantage of his announcement that he could now "kiss the new bride."

Enjoying his apparent embarrassment, Maura couldn't resist making the situation even more difficult for him.

"Luther," she sweetly implored, "didn't you hear the minister say that you could kiss me?" she asked, her eyelashes fluttering as she looked from the preacher back toward Luther, hoping he would feel an iota of the humiliation she was bearing due to his oafish attitude.

"I'm sorry. A kiss—is that what you're wanting?" he asked, the anger in his eyes directed at his new bride.

Immediately she knew she'd gone too far and had just opened her mouth to apologize when she felt her body being crushed against his. The fullness of his lips covered hers with a reckless intensity that left her breathless.

11-4-98

**JUDITH MCCOY MILLER** was chosen favorite new author in the Heartsong series, and her historical novels have ranked high among readers. In her first contemporary novel, *A Trusting Heart,* Judith drew on events in her own life to make the story come alive. Her other books draw from her fascination with history. She makes her home in Kansas with her family.

HEARTSONG PRESENTS

**Books by Judith McCoy Miller**
HP223—Threads of Love
HP244—Woven Threads
HP286—A Trusting Heart

# Changes
# of the Heart

*Judith McCoy Miller*

*Heartsong Presents*

**A note from the author:**

*I love to hear from my readers! You may correspond with me by writing:*

Judith McCoy Miller
Author Relations
PO Box 719
Uhrichsville, OH 44683

ISBN 1-57748-458-4

**CHANGES OF THE HEART**

*Cover illustration by Kathy Arbuckle.*

PRINTED IN THE U.S.A.

# prologue

## June 1847

"I suppose I'd be packing my bag and heading out of town, too, if I'd been left standing at the church. Folks hear tell of a bride that's left standing at the altar, but I don't believe I've ever heard of a groom being made the fool," Josiah Buchanan callously remarked to his son, Luther.

"I don't particularly think of myself as a fool, Father, but I realize that if I'm going to make anything of my life, I must leave you and this town," the younger man stated, not allowing his voice to betray the pain his father's words had caused.

"As usual, you're going to be late," his father continued to admonish, pulling the gold timepiece from his vest pocket and shaking his head. "After twenty-five years, I might as well just give up. Day after day I've told you that if you're ever going to amount to anything, you've got to be punctual. Why do you think I bought you that expensive pocket watch?"

"The stage doesn't arrive for another hour, and although you refrain from believing facts, I am seldom late for anything," Luther rebutted, wishing that his father would leave the room and allow him to complete packing his valise in solitude. But he knew that wouldn't happen. Until the stage door was closed and the horses were urged into motion, his father would be at his side, reminding him of his failures and berating him as a son.

"I just can't imagine what got into that girl. I went and talked to her parents, did I tell you that?" Josiah asked, ignoring Luther's remark.

"No, you didn't tell me, but I wish you hadn't done that. I'm

5

sure it only served to make them uncomfortable. It's not their fault that Elizabeth ran off with someone else."

"Well, she's their daughter. Her behavior decries their ability to rear a child. I told them that, too," Josiah pompously reported, his large belly puffing out even farther than usual. "Besides, I wasn't overly concerned about their discomfort. Look what I had to endure last Saturday when that little snippet didn't appear for the ceremony. Everyone expressing their sympathy and then laughing behind my back," the older man recounted as his thick neck reddened above his stiff white collar.

"This isn't about you, Father. If people are laughing, they're laughing at me. You can rest easy now. My departure should assure you that you've suffered your last embarrassment at my expense," Luther said, weary of the conversation and weary of his father's self-centered viewpoint.

"I still think you're making a mistake. Not about leaving Virginia, but going out west to California. Everyone's rushing out there thinking they're going to get rich overnight. Well, it doesn't happen that way. People get ahead by hard work, making sound decisions, and being punctual," Josiah lectured.

"I've already explained that I'm not going off in search of gold. I plan to open a mercantile store and perform the same services I've done in your business all these years," Luther reminded his father.

"Yes, so you've told me. Once you've set up your own store, you'll soon find that there is much you don't know about operating a business. You'll be racing home with your tail between your legs before two years have passed; that is my estimate. I'll hold your job for you," he promised, and then laughed heartily.

Luther knew it would serve no purpose to respond, but he vowed to himself that he would never return to his father's house. Since his mother's death fifteen years earlier, he had silently endured his father's sarcasm and tongue-lashings. Endured a childhood that had molded him into an angry man who already believed that he was destined to become a failure. Endured Elizabeth's recent rejection, which now served to reinforce what his father's behavior had taught him as a child—he was unlovable.

# one

## May 1852

Maura Rebecca Thorenson slipped her fingers into the serviceable brown leather bag she was carrying and touched the packet of letters nestled in its depths. They were carefully bound with a blue grosgrain ribbon, along with a new journal and the small Bible that had belonged to her grandmother. A shiver ran down her spine as she and her parents, Walt and Bessie Thorenson, stood on one of the docks scattered along Boston's harbor.

"You sure you're ready for this, Maura?" her father inquired, concern evident in his voice. His eyes remained fixed on the ship that she would board in a few short minutes.

"I'm not as sure as I was last week," she replied, laughing nervously. "Mama, I was only joking. Please don't cry anymore. This is my chance for a new life. We've been over this so many times that I thought you were finally in agreement," she said, leaning down to embrace her mother. Bessie was six inches shorter than her twenty-eight-year-old daughter, and it never seemed more evident than when the two women hugged each other. Maura had been blessed with the thick auburn hair of her father and the creamy complexion and blue eyes of her mother. Classic beauty, that's what her mother used to say—you have classic beauty, Maura. As a child she delighted in that particular compliment; but, as she developed into an adolescent, she decided classic beauty was not what interested boys.

"I've accepted the fact that you're leaving, Maura. Please don't ask me to remain dry eyed when my only daughter is leaving home. I'll probably never see you again," she answered between sobs, which then developed into a case of hiccoughs, causing both of them to giggle.

Walt and Bessie had been dismayed when Maura first informed them she had answered an ad for a mail-order bride. They had given her all the arguments against doing such a thing. Initially, she had conceded to their request that she not make a hasty decision, and when she wrote her letter of introduction to Luther Buchanan, she inquired if he would correspond with her for a year. Maura had carefully penned the letter, telling him of her life in Boston. She enclosed a photograph, as his advertisement had requested. It had been taken when she turned twenty-one years old, and although she didn't think she had aged much, she was careful to advise Mr. Buchanan the picture was seven years old.

Maura's parents had reasoned that a year would at least give their daughter an opportunity to become acquainted with this stranger's views and expectations for a wife. After receiving the letter and photograph of Maura, Luther had reluctantly agreed to wait for six months. Although more mail had been sent from Boston to Placerville, California, than the reverse, Luther Buchanan had kept his promise and answered all of the questions Maura listed in each of her letters to him. After several months of corresponding had elapsed, and without solicitation from Maura, Luther sent her a photograph of himself standing outside the Buchanan General Mercantile.

The picture had been taken at a distance and Luther's features were blurred, but Maura didn't care. She had never put much stock in physical attributes, which was the reason she hadn't requested a picture of her husband-to-be. It did appear that he was tall enough to overshadow Maura's height, but pictures could be as deceiving as actual appearances. Maura had learned early in life that some of the most attractive people could be the most disagreeable and thoughtless.

Having lived all her life in the same place, Maura found the prospect of moving to California as exciting as it was frightening. Maura had worked with her parents in their bookstore and bindery business since she was a young girl. During her school years, she and her brother, Dan, had been expected to spend at least two hours after school and all day Saturday helping in the family business. Daniel, three years her senior, had left home years ago. After attending Harvard, he'd read law under the tutelage of a highly respected Boston attorney and was eventually asked to become a partner in the practice. Married and the father of four small children, Dan and his family were frequent visitors at the Thorenson household. It was Amanda, Dan's wife, in whom Maura had confided her plan to answer the ad. And it was Amanda who had become her strongest advocate in persuading the senior Thorensons to agree.

After several hours of listening to the two women, her father had voiced his reservations about the arrangement but added that he realized Maura was certainly old enough to make her own decision to leave home and marry.

Later, after Luther had agreed to the six-month waiting period, Walt hadn't told his daughter that he felt compelled to make inquiries regarding the voyage she would be taking. After extensive investigation, her father had personally written to Luther Buchanan, setting forth what he considered mandatory arrangements before he would allow Maura to make the journey. Walt had somehow failed to advise his daughter of that information also.

Nor had he divulged all of his findings to his wife, Bessie, knowing she would become even more distraught about the situation. He was, however, inordinately forthright in describing the facts to Maura.

"You realize the journey could take up to eight months?" he'd asked her several days after returning from a trip to the docks.

"Luther wrote that some of the ships make the voyage in as few as four months. It just depends upon the weather, Father," she had responded.

"Did he also tell you about the bad food, seasickness, and boredom?"

"No, but I'm not a picky eater, and I'm sure I can pass the time reading and writing in my journal. As to seasickness, I suppose we'll be at the mercy of the weather and there's not much I can do about that."

"I realize you're not finicky about your meals, Maura. But I'm talking about concoctions of a stringy paste made from salted meat, potatoes, and hard bread, or something the sailors call hushamagrundy—made of turnips and parsnips with a bid of codfish thrown in. That's the good meals—before the supplies run low. When that occurs, they resort to three bean soup, which is mostly water, three beans, and a tiny piece of rusty pork. I was also told the water becomes foul after being stored in vats for several months. It attracts bugs and insects, and folks sometimes resort to adding vinegar and molasses just to kill the horrid taste. I'm not trying to discourage you, but I think you need to know what lies ahead," he'd told her.

"It sounds worse than I had imagined, but Luther said it was the best of the three options available. He said the trip overland was much more difficult, and he hadn't talked to anyone who recommended the sea-land-sea route across the Isthmus of Panama. I trust his judgment on sailing around the Cape."

"I trust his judgment on that also. I'm not suggesting that you change your route. But I talked at length to a sea captain who told me that if his daughter were making the trip, he'd not let her travel on any ship but the *Edward Everett*. It's a luxury ship that serves decent food and has excellent accommodations for its passengers. It is more expensive but more suited to genteel travelers," he'd explained.

"It does sound much more inviting, but Luther is planning on the voyage costing only five hundred dollars."

"If he wants you as a wife, I feel certain he will be more than willing to pay for you to travel in the most comfortable and respectable manner," Walt had replied.

"I suppose I could write to him, but I doubt the letter would reach him and give him enough time to send the additional funds before my departure date," she had thoughtfully explained to her father.

"No need to write. I did that some time ago."

"You wrote to Luther without telling me? What did you say?"

"I merely explained to him what I've just told you—along with the fact that he'd have to send the price of a ticket on the *Edward Everett,* or I'd not allow you to make the journey."

"Papa, how could you do that?" she had asked in a voice strained with anger.

"How could I not? You are my child, and no matter what your age, I have an obligation to seek what is best for your welfare. I couldn't live with myself if I did less than that," he had answered.

It was impossible for her to argue with such a reply. He had opened his arms, and she had willingly gone to him, returning his hug. It was during that moment she had realized more than ever before how much he loved her.

Luther had written to Walt, agreeing to pay for Maura's passage on the *Edward Everett.* Although he had made sure Walt knew the cost was more than double what he had planned, his willingness gave Walt a sense of confidence that Luther was a good man and one who would treat his daughter well.

"Now I know why the name of the ship sounds so familiar," Bessie remarked. "Walter, isn't the president of Harvard named Edward Everett?"

"Indeed he is. I'm told the ship was named after him,

although I'm not sure why. Perhaps the owner is a Harvard graduate. I feel certain, however, that Edward Everett wouldn't permit it to carry his name unless it was a fine vessel," he answered.

The crowds along the dock were beginning to swell. Some of the passengers were already aboard the ship, but Daniel and Amanda had not yet arrived with the children and Maura had no intention of leaving without bidding them good-bye. The gathering multitude of travelers and well-wishers were, for the most part, in jovial spirits. Mixed among them were a few teary-eyed women bidding their male companions farewell, as boisterous children raced between clustered groups of friends and family.

"There they are," Walter called out, waving his arms to signal his son and family. It took several long minutes for the group to wend their way through the throngs of people, but soon the children were circling around Maura, caught up in the excitement of the voyage.

"Can we go on board and see the ship, Aunt Maura?" asked Daniel, Jr., the oldest of Dan's children.

"I'm not sure. Let's go and ask," she said, leading the group toward the gangplank. As they reached their destination, she turned toward her brother. "Perhaps if you ask, they'll be more agreeable," she whispered.

Daniel nodded and moved forward. "Excuse me, sir. We've come to bid my sister farewell, and the children would like to board the ship to examine her accommodations. Would that be possible?" he politely inquired.

"I don't think I have the authority to give permission for that," the man hesitantly responded, though giving Daniel a wink.

"Would this help you obtain enough authority?" Daniel asked, slipping the man several coins.

The sailor glanced into his hand and smiled. "You folks enjoy yourselves. Just be sure and get off before we set sail.

Otherwise, you'll all end up in California," he said and then laughed, apparently amused at the statement.

Dan, Jr., and his brother, Samuel, led the group on board while the two girls clung closely to their mother and Maura. "Are you sure you want to go, Aunt Maura? How can you leave everything you know and go live with a stranger?" Ruth asked.

"Ruth! You have no business questioning your aunt's decision," Amanda reprimanded the girl.

"It's all right, Amanda. Why shouldn't she ask what everyone else I know has been wondering? Ruth, it's difficult to explain. I'm not sure beyond all doubt that this is what I should do. On the other hand, I've prayed about it and feel that my life in Boston is leading me nowhere and that God has a plan in mind for me elsewhere. It's going to be very difficult not having all of you around, and I hope one day your parents will take the time to come and visit. I've tried to think I'll see all of you again, but I know there is a strong possibility that may not happen. I'm going to have to depend upon you, your mother, and grandmother to keep me posted on all the news. Do you think you could help with that?"

"Yes, I'll write to you, but what happens if you don't like this man you're supposed to marry?" she asked, not relenting in her pursuit of answers.

"Well, his letters have revealed that he's a Christian man and that he's anxious for my arrival. If I don't like him, I'll have to depend on God to give me a change of heart."

"But what if He doesn't?" Ruth insisted while Jenny, the youngest of the four children, clung to Amanda's skirt.

"Then I suppose He'll do something else to change my circumstances. I'm not trying to escape answering your questions, dear. I just don't know the answers," her aunt replied, smiling at the girl.

"Thank you for trying, Aunt Maura. I want you to be happy, and I'm sure God will take care of everything. After all, He knows how special you are," Ruth said, wrapping her arms around her aunt's waist.

Amanda smiled over her daughter's head into Maura's eyes. "Did you tell him?" she whispered to Maura.

Maura moved her head back and forth negatively and mouthed the word no to her sister-in-law.

"Ruth, why don't you take Jenny and the two of you go find the rest of the family and tell them we've located Aunt Maura's quarters? Ask them to come along and join us," she instructed.

The two women watched as the girl left the cabin and skipped down the passageway on her assigned mission.

"Maura, I can't believe you didn't tell him. Each time I asked, you told me you were going to in your next letter," Amanda stated accusingly.

"I meant to, Amanda, truly I did. But the longer I put it off, the more difficult it became. I was afraid he'd ask why I hadn't told him when I originally answered his ad. Then, as time passed, I didn't want to tell him for fear he'd be angry and break the engagement," she explained, holding back the tears that threatened to spill over at any minute.

"I'm sorry, Maura. I didn't mean to make you unhappy," Amanda replied, giving her a quick hug. "I'm sure it will be fine. How could he not love you? You're the finest person I've ever known—except perhaps for your brother," she quickly added.

Maura smiled weakly. "Please don't tell my parents. They think Luther knows and has accepted my 'affliction,' as they call it."

"I won't mention it. Just promise that when you write to me, you will tell me the truth about your new life," her sister-in-law pleaded.

"I'm sure that everything will be wonderful and my letters will overflow with only good news to all of you. However, should something arise that I don't want the others to know,

I'll send along a separate page addressed just to you. I trust you'll not reveal the information to anyone."

"You have my word," Amanda replied solemnly.

"It makes me feel better just knowing I'll have a confidante should I need one," Maura said optimistically, attempting to ignore the twinge of doubt lurking deep inside her heart.

"You two certainly appear to be deep in conversation," Daniel commented as he walked into the cabin followed by the rest of the family. "I don't think we'll all fit in here at once, children. Why don't you wait until we've looked around and then you can come in," Daniel instructed the excited youngsters.

"It's awfully small, dear. Do you think you'll be able to live in this tiny space for eight months?" her mother inquired, her concerns obviously not assuaged by their tour of the vessel.

"Mother, I won't be confined to my cabin," she rebutted.

"Of course, she won't," her father interjected. "Bessie, you've talked to almost every member of the ship's crew. She'll have weekly papers to read, and there are concerts to attend as well as a variety of other activities. There's a board of health and a police department should she have medical problems or need protection of any sort. This room is elegant, and the bill of fare sounds better than what most of the Boston restaurants serve. You must quit your fretting," he admonished.

"I know, I know, but it doesn't make it any easier to see her leave home," Bessie responded.

"Let's allow the children to see her cabin," Walt suggested, changing the subject and moving his wife toward the door.

"You're next," Walt said to the children as he and his wife exited the cabin.

"It's as beautiful as I told you, isn't it?" Ruth asked her sister as they entered the room.

"Oh, yes," her younger sister agreed, her voice filled with awe. "I wish I could come with you, Aunt Maura," Emily added. "I would be happy forever in this room."

"I seriously doubt that, Emily," her father said. "You grow tired of everything within a few hours. Just imagine if you had to stay on this ship for six months. I think you would probably change your mind."

"Your father is right, Emily. Although the room and ship are lovely, I'm sure the trip will be long and sometimes very boring. I would love to have your company on the voyage, but I think you'll be much happier playing outdoors with your friends all summer rather than being a captive on this ship," Maura told the child.

Walter poked his head just inside the door of the cabin. "We've got to leave the ship now. They're about ready to set sail."

All of them quickly gathered together and moved with the other visitors toward the gangplank. Maura followed along with them, a sense of fear beginning to creep into her consciousness. Now that the time of departure had finally arrived, she didn't want them to know she was filled with anxiety. Pasting a smile on her face, she hugged each of them and watched as they walked down the gangplank and back to the dock. As the ship slowly moved out of its berth, she stood transfixed on the deck while attempting to emblazon a picture of each of them in her mind. The minutes passed, and their figures became smaller and smaller until they were no longer in view. She could neither force herself to move from the railing nor take her eyes from the spot where she had last seen her family's waving arms. Nothing but water remained in sight, but she held her vigil until the sun began to set.

# two

Despite her fears and new surroundings, Maura slept soundly. She awoke the next morning just as the sun was rising and peeked out her cabin window. The scene was beyond expectation. The sun appeared as a blazing ball rising out of the water and the sky a mixture of soft aquamarine and burnished red dipping down to meet the bluish-black depths of the ocean. She continued to revel in the sight until her growling stomach served as a reminder she had not eaten since departing the previous day. Although a light evening meal had been offered, Maura had preferred to remain at the ship's railing staring toward the beauty of a distant horizon. Now, almost twenty-four hours since her last meal, she realized she was famished.

Deciding upon a white muslin dress with a pattern of roses scattered about the border, Maura prepared herself for her first full day at sea. Weeks earlier, her mother had hand stitched the three-tier skirt, each layer emphasizing the delicate rose-patterned border. The bodice was a fashionable V-neckline exhibiting a modest inset of white embroidered muslin. Gathering her auburn tresses in a pale green ribbon that complemented the green leaves in her dress, Maura decided upon carrying her green silk parasol. It would provide her creamy complexion ample protection from the sun, should she decide to linger on deck after breakfast.

"Are you going to the dining room?" a voice called out. Maura turned to see a small, white-haired woman walking toward her.

"Yes, I've not eaten since we set sail, and my stomach is beginning to protest," Maura responded, observing no one

18

else in their vicinity and assuming the woman was address-ing her.

"Would you mind very much if I joined you? I can't tolerate eating by myself, and it seems most of the passengers are men who prefer talking to each other rather than an old woman. I'm Rachel Windsor," she said, extending her hand as she reached Maura's side.

"And I'm Maura Thorenson. I would be delighted to have your company at breakfast," she replied while walking along-side the older woman.

"I'll try not to bore you to tears or make a nuisance of myself, although I'm sure you'll be glad to see the last of me once we reach California," Rachel stated as they entered the dining room.

"Where are you going?" Rachel asked as Maura moved toward one of the large dining tables.

"To seat myself at one of the tables," she answered, giving the elder woman a questioning look.

"I forgot that you weren't at dinner last evening. We serve ourselves," Rachel explained. "The food is placed on that large table close to the kitchen," she said, pointing toward the far side of the room.

Maura hadn't noticed the line of people waiting at the other side of the room and was embarrassed when she noticed sev-eral passengers staring at the two of them. Hesitating for a moment, she placed her parasol on one of the benches and moved with Rachel to the end of the line.

"Do you need assistance? I can fill my plate and come back for yours," Rachel offered.

"No, I'm more than capable of taking care of myself," Maura answered more sharply than she'd intended. Noting the look of remorse on Rachel's face, she quickly apolo-gized. "I didn't mean to be so abrupt. I'm sorry if I hurt your feelings."

"You don't owe me an apology, Maura," Rachel replied.

"Now, let's see what they're serving for breakfast," she added as they reached the table.

After helping themselves to generous portions of ham, eggs, biscuits, fresh fruit, and steaming cups of coffee, the women seated themselves at the table where Maura had earlier placed her parasol.

"As far as I'm concerned, these tables certainly make eating difficult," Rachel said to those seated close by. "I understand the need for this edge around the table, but you'd think someone would invent one that could be removed when the seas are calm," she complained.

"Know what you mean," the man seated across from them agreed. "By the end of the meal, my arms feel as though they have permanent dents in them."

"Perhaps you should try lifting your arm to your mouth instead of leaning over your plate," the woman to his left sarcastically responded.

"You're not my mother, and I don't need your advice on how to eat," he shot back in a churlish tone.

"I didn't mean to start a feud," Rachel interjected. "If the sunrise is any indication, it looks as though there's a beautiful day awaiting us," she continued, hoping that the couple would cease their bickering.

"Think I'll see if I can find a game of cards," the man replied, picking up his plate and rising.

"It's a little early in the day for you to begin your gambling, isn't it?" his companion queried.

"I'll be glad when we get to Rio de Janeiro," he mumbled as he walked away from the table.

"Let's hope you haven't lost all of our money before we get there," she called after him.

Obviously unflappable, the woman offered no apology or explanation to those remaining at the dining table. Instead, she picked up her fork and continued the meal as though nothing out of the ordinary had occurred.

Rachel remained somewhat subdued for the remainder of the meal. Maura tried to engage her in conversation several times, but Rachel would give a brief answer and offer nothing further. Finally Maura gave up and ate in silence, relieved when the meal was finally completed.

"I believe I'll gather my writing materials and return to the deck. It's such a beautiful morning, and I want to add a few paragraphs to the letter I'm writing my sister-in-law and make notations in my journal," she commented as they reached her cabin.

"I believe I'll read in my room for a while. I think I've stirred up enough trouble for one day," she replied.

"Rachel, that wasn't your fault. Those two obviously fight all the time. It was apparent they had no respect for each other or the rest of us, for that matter," she comforted her new acquaintance.

"You're probably right, but I still feel uncomfortable for any part I played in that altercation," she answered. "Perhaps I'll join you later this morning. If not, I'll see you at dinner."

Maura watched the older woman stride down the passage-way, head held high, shoulders thrown back, a picture of determination and self-reliance. No one would guess she was retreating to her room for any reason other than a brief respite after her morning meal.

The days soon became a monotonous routine, and had it not been for Rachel and Georgette Blackburn, Maura couldn't have imagined how she could bear another three months aboard ship. Rachel's penchant to discuss literature, philosophy, and spiritual matters and Georgette's carefree disposition had proved advantageous to all three of them. Georgette, with her oval face, full cheeks, pouty lips, and lush blond curls, never failed to coax them into laughter. Her flair for making a humorous story out of everything offset Rachel's sober, reflective manner.

But even the intermittent concerts and literary discussion

groups became tiresome after a while, with most of the passengers preferring gambling to a scholarly conversation about the literary genius of Shakespeare or Chaucer.

❧

Maura stepped from her cabin, planning to join Georgette for a few hours of visiting, but she quickly returned for her woolen cape and bonnet.

"It has certainly turned cold, hasn't it?" she remarked to one of the crew members who was walking down the passageway as she gathered the warm cape tightly around her.

"It will only get worse," he casually remarked.

"What do you mean?" she asked, somewhat surprised by his reply.

"It may be summer in New England, but it's winter where we're headed. The closer we get to the Cape, the colder and rougher the weather becomes. Didn't anyone tell you that before you left home?" he asked, obviously surprised at her lack of knowledge.

"Nobody I know has made this voyage," she replied.

"Who you going to meet in California?" he asked.

"I'm getting married. My husband-to-be is in California."

"Seems he would have told you what to expect," he commented, continuing on his way.

"What do you mean—what to expect?" she questioned, walking as quickly as her handicap would permit.

"Like I said, it's winter down here. The winds get bad; the temperature gets frigid; and stormy seas are the general fare. Sorry, but I don't have time to talk. The first mate's waiting on me," he replied, scurrying off and leaving her with a multitude of unanswered questions.

Casting her head downward against the harsh wind, she finally arrived at Georgette's cabin and pounded on the thick wooden door. "Georgette," she called out, "hurry, it's cold out here!"

When Georgette finally opened the door, Maura rushed

inside, the cold biting at her hands and feet. "I can't believe how quickly the weather has turned on us," she said, rubbing her hands together. When she finally looked up, she saw why Georgette had been so slow to answer.

"Georgette, what's wrong? You look positively dreadful," Maura said, noticing the girl's sallow complexion and shaking hands.

"I think I'd better lie down for a while. Suddenly, I'm feeling. . ." Georgette winced as though she were in pain and fell upon the bed.

"Feeling what?" Maura coaxed.

Georgette didn't immediately answer and Maura's concern heightened when she noted the girl's swollen belly.

"Georgette! Are you going to have a baby?" Maura asked, stunned that she hadn't previously realized the girl was pregnant.

"Yes," she feebly replied. "I've kept it well hidden, haven't I? I bet you and Rachel wondered why I was always wearing a long cape around me, even on those horribly warm days, didn't you?"

"I assumed you were cold-natured, Georgette. You told me you weren't married, and quite honestly, I never gave a thought to the idea that you might be expecting a child. As for Rachel, she has never mentioned your attire and speaks only good of you," Maura answered.

"It doesn't matter. I don't know how I thought I could keep this a secret until we arrived in California anyway," Georgette said, her voice growing weaker.

"When is your baby due?" Maura asked, taking hold of Georgette's hand.

"Not for another ten weeks. I'm so afraid, Maura. Please don't leave me," she pleaded.

"I won't leave, but I think we should try and get you into your nightgown and under the covers. I've always heard bed rest was the best thing if there was fear the baby would be premature," she explained, remembering the difficulties Amanda had encountered during her last pregnancy. Maura had stayed with Daniel and Amanda during that trying time when her sister-in-law had been required to remain in bed for ten weeks. It had been worth it, however, when after those long boring days of lying in bed Amanda had given birth to a healthy, beautiful daughter—sweet little Jenny.

Digging deeply into one of Georgette's trunks, she found a warm nightgown; and after what seemed like an eternity, her young friend was tucked into bed. The cramping had finally subsided, and Georgette slipped into a restless sleep under Maura's watchful eyes.

Several hours later, Georgette awakened and found Maura sitting beside her bed reading a small Bible.

"I'm feeling much better," she announced. "The pain seems to have completely gone away. I'm sorry to have frightened you, but I think it was a false alarm."

"Perhaps, but I think it would be best if you remained in bed for at least the next several days. I'll see that your meals are brought to your cabin and explain to Rachel you're just a bit under the weather," she stated firmly.

"But what if Rachel wants to come and visit? I don't want her to know I'm pregnant. What will she think of me? She knows I'm not married—or even engaged, for that matter. I feel somewhat stronger, and it will be better if I just try to carry on as I have been."

"Absolutely not! If you care nothing about yourself, think of what damage you may do to the unborn child if you don't take care of yourself. I can handle Rachel, and if and when the time comes that she insists upon visiting you, we'll make advance arrangements so that your condition will be hidden from her view. I'll not argue about this, Georgette."

"You're not my mother! What makes you think you can tell me what I must do?" the younger girl retorted, angry that Maura was determined to have her way.

"It's certainly a fact I'm not your mother, but I'm as close to any female assistance as you'll find when it comes time to have your child. Besides, you know I'm only doing what's best for the two of you," Maura responded.

Georgette was quiet for several minutes, and Maura rose from the chair and picked up her bonnet and cape.

"Where are you going? I haven't gotten out of bed. I'll do whatever you think is best. Really I will, I promise."

Georgette couldn't see the smile that crossed Maura's face. "I'm going to go and get us something to eat. Do you think you can keep down a meal, or would you prefer just a bowl of soup?"

"I know this will probably surprise you, but I'm ravenous," Georgette replied with a sheepish grin.

"That's a good sign. I'll see what I can do about solving that problem. You stay in bed so nothing happens while I'm gone," she instructed the girl.

Fortunately, Rachel and the other passengers hadn't arrived for dinner when Maura entered the dining room. Spotting one of the cooks coming from the kitchen, she crossed the room as swiftly as possible and approached him.

"Excuse me, but would it be possible for me to have two trays prepared and delivered to Miss Blackburn's cabin?"

"Dinner won't be ready for another half hour, but I'll have the trays delivered before we begin serving. If the winds become any stronger, you may want to keep to your cabin after dinner. May turn into a rough night from the looks of things," he told her.

"Thank you, I'll keep that in mind. Is there any reason for concern?" she queried.

"Nothing out of the ordinary. The closer we get to the Cape, the worse the weather is this time of year. We'll be in for quite a ride over the next week or so," he explained.

"But you've never had a problem with this ship while round-ing the Cape, have you?"

"There's not a ship that doesn't have problems rounding Cape Horn in the middle of winter. But if you're asking if you think we're going to go down at sea, the answer would be no," he said with a benevolent smile.

Returning to Georgette's quarters, Maura thought perhaps the ship seemed to be rocking more arduously. *Now stop that,* she chastised herself. *You're allowing your thoughts to be controlled by a simple cautionary comment.*

By the time dinner arrived, there was no doubt that they had entered rougher waters. When Maura opened the door, the cabin boy tumbled into the room, somehow managing to keep their food within the confines of the covered trays while overcoming the obstacles of a lurching ship and Georgette's open trunk sitting just inside the doorway. He wasted no time depositing the items, bidding them good night, and scurrying back to the passageway.

"Let's see what's on the trays," Georgette said, plumping several pillows behind her and wiggling into a sitting position.

"Are you sure you want to eat? This turbulence has caused me to lose my appetite completely," Maura said, eyeing the girl in disbelief.

"Not me. I could eat a cow," Georgette replied and then giggled at her own remark.

Maura smiled weakly, feeling as though she would retch when the smell of the food reached her nostrils.

"Oh, how wonderful," Georgette said, sounding like a small child at Christmas. "Roast pork and potatoes. Oh, look, Maura, there's even apple pie with cheese for dessert. I can't remember the last time I had roast pork."

Moving across the room to avoid smelling the food, Maura positioned herself in a high-backed chair with cushioned arms and leaned her head back.

"This is delicious, Maura. Can I have your pie if you're not going to eat it?"

Closing her eyes, Maura nodded her head and leaned back.

Several minutes passed, and it seemed that the bow of the ship was going to touch the very depths of the ocean before it rose back up and violently descended in the opposite direction.

"Are you going to bring me the other tray, or should I get up?" Georgette ventured when Maura remained in the chair.

Her eyes fluttered open. "You're not to get up, and I'm not bringing you anything else to eat right now, Georgette," Maura responded just as the prow of the ship took yet another dive into the swirling waters.

"It's getting rather exciting, isn't it?" came Georgette's enthusiastic retort as the tray she had balanced on her bed went crashing to the floor, scraps of food and dishes tumbling helter-skelter.

Maura attempted to rise, but the swooping motion of the ship immediately threw her back into the chair.

"You're positively green, Maura. It seems strange, doesn't it? Just a short time ago I was the one in need of medical attention; but now, I believe, you are in worse condition than I was."

"Our ailments are completely dissimilar, Georgette. I am suffering from seasickness due to this horrendous weather. As soon as the weather clears, I'll be fine. Your ailment, however, won't disappear with the passing of a storm," Maura stated, irritated by the girl's comparison of seasickness with the possibility of a premature birth.

Seeing Georgette's pained look, Maura immediately regretted the outburst. "I'm sorry, Georgette. I didn't mean to hurt your feelings, but why don't you rest while you can and I'll do the same," she apologized, mustering a small smile.

"Papa always did tell me God must have given me a double helping of good looks to make up for my lack of common sense. I'll be quiet as a church mouse, and I'm sure that we'll both be feeling wonderful by morning," Georgette replied, making certain the railing on the bed was secure before turning to a more comfortable position.

During the next four days the weather roared with a violence that neither of them could have imagined. One of the crew members had come to Georgette's cabin the second day and told them to remain there and one of the crew would deliver what food he could as the weather permitted. Maura was unable to eat anything during the four days but did force herself to drink liquids to keep from dehydrating. Georgette, however, remained the epitome of good health and devoured every morsel of food each crew member delivered to the room.

The seas finally calmed, although the weather remained frigid for another week, but at least Maura was able to return to her cabin and assume a somewhat normal routine. One of her first priorities had been to find Rachel and see how she had fared throughout the storm. Discovering her cabin unoccupied, Maura had gone to the dining room and then the library in search of the older woman. Failing to locate her, Maura had finally inquired of the ship's captain, who revealed Rachel had come out on the deck during the storm, appearing to be delirious. Before any of the crew members could reach Rachel, she had been swept overboard.

"Our attempts to save her or recover her body went unrewarded."

Seeing Maura's hand rise to her mouth in shock as he related the horrible tale, he offered his regrets. "Were you related to her?" he inquired.

"No, no, but she was a lovely lady. We had just met on the ship, but I felt as though I'd known her for some time."

He nodded his understanding. "Do you know if there is someone I should notify—a family member in California, perhaps? We found nothing in her belongings to indicate why she was aboard the ship or if she had family elsewhere," he informed her.

"She told me that her family was all deceased and she wanted a bit of adventure in her life before she died. Having heard stories of the excitement in California, she decided to sell her home and move west. Apparently she was known for her excellent cooking and was planning to open a restaurant when she reached her new home," Maura told him, with Rachel's words still ringing in her memory.

"I'm sorry she didn't live to see her dream through. Since you're probably the closest thing she had to a relative, why don't you take her belongings when we get to California? She'd probably prefer that over my men scavenging through them."

Maura nodded. She wasn't sure she wanted to claim the belongings of a deceased woman she barely knew, but any further discussion of the subject seemed abhorrent.

Slowly making her way back to Georgette's cabin, Maura wrestled with thoughts of how to break the news to her young friend. The three of them had grown close during the voyage, and although Georgette was somewhat intimidated by Rachel's maturity and sophistication, her respect for the older woman's Christian standards and beliefs was obvious. While Maura and Rachel studied and discussed passages of scripture, Georgette would often sit nearby listening intently. In turn, Rachel always attempted to draw Georgette into their Bible studies.

"Her questions make it apparent she's trying to find what's missing in her life. I hope somehow I can play a small part in helping her find it," Rachel had once confided to Maura.

Maura was pleased that Rachel had found that opportunity and led Georgette to the Lord. Rachel could have taught Georgette so much more about God's love, Maura sadly thought as she entered the doorway.

"Did you visit with Rachel while you were gone? How did she make it through the storm?" Georgette asked the minute Maura entered the cabin.

"Not very well, I'm afraid. You see. . ."

"Did you tell her about the baby? What did she say? Do you think she'll ever speak to me again? Oh, I hope so; I hope she'll find it in her heart to forgive me. What's wrong, Maura? You look positively ill. I'm sorry. Here I am just rambling on with my questions and you're sick. Why don't you sit down and rest? Can I get you something?"

"Georgette, I don't know how to say this, so I'll just come straight out with it. Rachel died during the storm. The captain told me she had come up on deck during the squall. Apparently she was ill and had become delirious. She was hit with a giant wave and washed overboard. They weren't able to save her."

"No! That can't be true. Surely they've made some mistake, Maura. Tell me this isn't so," the girl pleaded in a trembling voice.

"I wish I could, but there's no way to change the truth," Maura replied.

"She told me once that she didn't fear death because time on earth was only a short delay on the path to eternity and that she was looking forward to heaven. I wish I could feel that way; but whenever I think about death, I still become frightened," Georgette mused.

"As you grow in your faith you'll find that same assurance," Maura encouraged.

"I hope so, but it's difficult for me to remember that God has forgiven all the terrible things I've done in my life. Somehow it just seems too simple to ask for forgiveness and receive it. Look at what my family did to me when I asked for their forgiveness! They sent me off to California so that they wouldn't be humiliated. It's truly amazing that God will forgive me when my own flesh and blood has disowned me!"

"But don't you see, Georgette—your parents are human— just like you and me. You can't compare them to God and His perfect love. I know it seems too simple that this gift is ours, free for the taking. Perhaps that's why so many reject it—because it is a sovereign gift, straight from God through His Son," Maura replied.

"I'm just thankful that God sent you and Rachel into my life to explain all of this. Had I remained at home with my family, I may have never accepted the Lord. Perhaps one day I'll have the opportunity to lead someone else—maybe even someone in my family," Georgette quietly reflected.

# three

"So you're finally off to San Francisco to get your woman. I was beginning to think it was. . ."

"Was what? A lie?" Luther retorted, a sharp edge to his voice.

The two old men had been sitting in the corner of the store playing cards all afternoon, just as they did most afternoons. The only difference between today and the countless other afternoons was the fact that they were taking great pleasure in baiting the proprietor about his approaching marriage.

"Don't get yourself all riled up, Luther. You know Aaron's only funnin' with ya."

"I'm tired of listening to both of you. If you want to sit and play cards, that's fine. But don't sit in my store and call me a liar."

"I'm sorry, Luther. Hank's right, ya know. I'd never call you a liar. You're a good man, and I wish you only the best," Aaron apologized, running his fingers through the gray, scruffy beard that surrounded his haggard face.

"We'd best be getting out of your way," Hank commented, nudging the other man to get up.

"Oh, yeah, we got things to do. We'll see ya when you get back from San Francisco," Aaron called over his shoulder as the two men made their way toward the doorway of the Buchanan Mercantile.

"Sorry, Aaron. I'm just a little nervous—don't hold it against me," Luther replied, giving a half-hearted wave at the men. "Great! At this rate, I won't need to come back to Placerville. I'll have run off all my customers," he muttered aloud, checking the shelves one last time.

He disliked leaving the store, but going to San Francisco to pick up supplies was a necessity, and he didn't trust anyone else with that chore. He'd learned that it took a careful eye to avoid having one's cargo shorted. There were always beggars and thieves on the wharf, men down on their luck as well as those who were too lazy to work for a living. They prowled among the cargo as it was unloaded, helping themselves to anything they could carry off. Shortly after his arrival, he'd traveled to the docks to collect his first shipment of goods. To his amazement, several thieves had been successful in joining forces and hauling off large crates while the unwitting crew was aboard ship fetching the remaining cargo. From that day forward, Luther made every effort to be present on the wharf when his cargo was being unloaded, and he didn't leave until it was completely accounted for and secured.

He had carefully devised a plan to successfully protect his cargo and haul it to Placerville. After inquiring about various ships' captains, he engaged Captain Nedrick Wharton, a man of good reputation, to transport his supplies. Captain Wharton had delivered all of the cargo for the Buchanan Mercantile for the past five years. The two men had a gentlemen's agreement that Luther's cargo was never to be unloaded until his arrival at the dock, and, in exchange, Captain Wharton would receive several gold coins for the added service. The process had worked admirably, and Luther could boast that no thief had ever pilfered any of his stock.

Likewise, Luther had made painstaking arrangements with a local livery where he boarded his horses and wagon while in the city. He would rent two additional wagons and drivers to assist in hauling the supplies back to Placerville. The drivers varied from trip to trip, but the owner of the livery vouched for any man he hired out, and Luther had never met with any complications.

His attention to detail and unfaltering determination to disprove his father's prediction of failure had caused a transformation. From an insecure, yet trusting human being, Luther had slowly evolved into a man with a penchant for success and a lack of tolerance for obstacles that might delay his achievements.

As his business flourished in the small gold mining town, Luther had realized that an extra pair of hands would allow him to move even more rapidly toward achieving his goals. And, in his methodical calculations, he came to the conclusion that the best way to gain another pair of hands was to marry. There were abundant benefits to the plan. Aside from the obvious advantage, he would have additional help without the added expense. Granted, he would have to feed and clothe a wife, but that would cost less than hiring a full-time employee. Besides, he would no longer be required to send out his laundry or cook his own meals; he could train her to balance the ledgers, a chore he despised; and, as she bore children, there would be even more hands to help! The only problem would be finding a woman. California was overpopulated with men, but women—at least good Christian women—were nowhere to be found. In order to resolve his problem, Luther had once again devised a plan.

It had been a little over a year ago when he had traveled to San Francisco and requested Captain Wharton deliver his advertisement to the East Coast for publication in several newspapers. The responses had been less than he had hoped for—one from a woman almost twice his age, another from a married woman wanting to escape a cruel husband, and one from Maura Thorenson. Although Miss Thorenson came the closest to meeting his requirements, he wasn't entirely satisfied. In her first letter, she avowed to be twenty-eight years old. He would have preferred a woman of eighteen or nineteen years of age, young and healthy, who could earn her keep and give him many children. But at least she appeared in good health and somewhat comely in the picture she had sent.

Of course, the request by the woman's parents that she correspond with him for an entire year before setting sail for California had been totally unacceptable. He had begrudgingly conceded to a six-month delay, arguing that his bride's traveling time of at least six months would require him to wait over a year for her arrival in San Francisco. Throughout the six-month correspondence period, he had continued to hope that some younger, more suitable prospect would contact him and be willing to make immediate arrangements to marry him. Those hopes had heightened even further when Luther received a letter from Walter Thorenson practically demanding that his precious daughter travel aboard a luxury ship to California. Luther was aghast as he had calculated the additional cost, but he had bleakly agreed when he was unable to devise a logical plan to avoid the request. If Mr. Thorenson thought him a miser, he'd likely entice Maura to cancel their wedding. And Luther didn't want that to occur!

Now, after a year of anticipating the arrival of his bride, Luther was leaving Placerville as a single man for the last time. When he returned, he would have a wife—a helpmeet.

"I'll expect an accounting of everything when I return," Luther admonished the man he had hired to look after the store during his absence. "As usual, I've completed an inventory of all the merchandise, so I'll know if you attempt anything underhanded."

"The preacher vouched for me, Mr. Buchanan. I'm an honest man, and I worked in the general store in my hometown for ten years before coming to California. We've been over this for the past two weeks. If you don't trust me, find someone else to tend the place," Clem Halbert rebutted.

"I'm sorry, Clem. It's just that I don't like leaving my business in the hands of someone else. Every time I go to San Francisco, I've got this problem. Used to be Johnny Weber would take care of things, and I was finally getting used to him. Now that he's up and left, it's, well—"

"I understand, Luther, but you got two choices. Either trust the store to me or stay home. Makes me no difference at this point. Course, if you decide to stay in Placerville, I may ride down to San Francisco and see if I can talk your intended into marrying me," he joked.

Luther laughed weakly in return. "Never know, she just might marry you if that happened. Women been known to reject a man for less!"

"Aw, ain't no woman gonna jilt you, Luther. She's coming halfway around the world to marry you. Now, you better get going before the sun's any farther up in the sky."

After checking the store one last time, he hoisted himself onto the seat of the wooden freight wagon and slapped the reins. "Giddyup," he called out as the horses slowly moved away from the front of the store.

❧

Georgette and Maura stood on the deck of the ship as it slowly maneuvered between the multitude of vessels in the San Francisco harbor, many of them in a terrible state of disrepair, obviously having been deserted for a long period of time.

"Why are all those ships in the harbor in such dreadful condition?" Maura asked one of the crew members who passed behind them.

"Them? Oh, once they dock, the sailors get gold fever and never return. The ships remain in the harbor until the captain can hire another crew. But that doesn't happen very often, so the ships sit here and rot," he explained. "You'll find some of them have been towed and placed between other buildings. They're used as hotels and general stores or saloons—looks strange at first, but you get used to it. I better get back to work."

"So you think your Luther Buchanan will be waiting on the dock?" Georgette asked.

"I really don't know. He said if he wasn't at the dock, I

should stay at the Ashton Hotel," she replied while attempting to calm what felt like a million butterflies encamped in her stomach.

"Are you frightened?" Georgette asked. "I know I would be. Marrying some complete stranger, not knowing if he'd like the way I look or act," she rambled on. "Does he know about that?" she asked, nodding her heard toward Maura's left side.

"No. I didn't think it was important," she responded defensively.

Georgette looked at her friend in astonishment. "Do you really believe that?" she asked, staring deeply into Maura's blue eyes.

"Why is it that everyone thinks the most important thing about me is the fact that I was born with a withered arm and leg, that I walk with a limp and have difficulty using my left hand? Is that any more important than the color of my hair or how much I weigh—or perhaps how tall I am?" Maura countered angrily.

"Did you tell him the color of your hair and how tall you are?" Georgette quietly inquired.

"Yes, but only because he asked," came Maura's abrupt retort.

"I don't suppose it entered his mind to explore the possibility of some infirmity. He probably assumed you would have been candid about anything like that."

"Well, it makes no difference to me if he has an ailment of some type, so I didn't think there was any need to address the matter," Maura stated, squaring her shoulders as if ready to do battle. "There's nothing I can do to change my appearance. I was born this way and have had to deal with it all my life."

"Please don't misunderstand. I know that once Mr. Buchanan gets to know you, he won't even notice that you're. . ."

"Different?" Maura asked.

"Yes, different. You know you're different, and so do I. But once people get to know you, they no longer notice. I just thought you would tell Mr. Buchanan so that he would be prepared to accept you as you are. Oh, no matter what I say, it comes out wrong," Georgette declared, her exasperation evident as she watched the ominous look crossing Maura's face.

"The fact is, he doesn't know that I'm crippled and it's too late to tell him now. But you're right—I was afraid he'd reject me if he knew," Maura admitted. "Guess I'll find out just what's important to him in the next hour or so."

The passengers were beginning to disembark when the captain rushed over to where Maura and Georgette were standing in line.

"I had my men place the other trunks with yours. They'll be together on the dock," he said. "Hope the trip wasn't totally unbearable, ladies. We strive to provide the finest service and consider ourselves a luxury ship, unlike most of those," he said, indicating toward the other ships in the harbor. "Unfortunately, we have no control over the weather, although it wasn't too bad this voyage," he finished.

Maura extended her thanks and kept her thoughts about the storm to herself, hoping she'd never again have to endure such horrid weather. Meanwhile, Georgette rattled on about how exciting the trip had been, apparently forgetting that her unborn child had threatened to make an early delivery. Maura had been surprised and extremely thankful that the girl had suffered no further difficulty with the pregnancy. By now there was no hiding her impending condition, and by Georgette's calculations, the baby had been due the previous week.

The two women walked arm-in-arm down the unsteady gangplank, Maura keeping her eyes on Georgette, not wanting a last-minute disaster. When they finally reached the firmness of the dock, Maura spied a man holding a picture and peering among the passengers who had disembarked. Leading Georgette in his direction, she took a closer look.

The man resembled the picture of Luther Buchanan, but she couldn't be sure.

She watched as he caught sight of them. His eyes darted back and forth between the two women and then slowly moved up and down the length of her. He was holding her picture in his hand, looking at the picture and then at her. For several minutes he didn't say anything; he just stared.

"Who's she?" were his first words.

"Georgette Blackburn. Georgette, I believe this is Luther Buchanan," Maura stated.

"Pleased to meet you. Maura and I met on the ship. She's such a wonderful lady that I don't know what I would have done without her. You're very fortunate she's agreed to be your wife, but I suppose you already know—"

"Georgette, you need not extol my virtues to Mr. Buchanan. You are Luther Buchanan, aren't you?" Maura interrupted.

"Of course, I'm Luther," he replied, his eyes resting on her left arm. "I've been here two days waiting on the ship and already made arrangements with the preacher and rented a room at the hotel. We'll leave in a couple days after I've gotten all my supplies loaded," he stated matter-of-factly. "Where's your belongings?"

Maura pointed out her trunks as well as those that had belonged to Rachel. Without any further comment, he nodded and hoisted them one by one onto a wagon.

"He doesn't seem to talk much, does he?" Georgette whispered just as Luther returned.

"Someone coming for you?" he asked Georgette.

"No, I don't think so," Georgette answered.

"What's that mean—you don't think so? Either you got someone coming or you don't," he bluntly retorted.

Maura saw tears begin to form in Georgette's eyes and answered for the girl. "There is no one meeting her. She's come to California to begin a new life."

"Looks to me like she's running away from her old life,"

Luther replied, obviously referring to Georgette's condition. "If you want a ride to the hotel, you can come with us," he offered in a voice devoid of any warmth.

"That would be very nice of you. Those are my trunks," Georgette meekly replied.

Maura thought she heard him make a comment under his breath, but she chose to ignore it. Although the hotel wasn't far, the escalating tenseness among the three passengers made the short trip seem like hours. Luther helped Georgette down and then reached up to assist Maura.

"We need to talk about that," he whispered, indicating toward the left side of her body.

Maura felt herself stiffen and quickly moved away from him. The two women walked into the hotel, followed by Luther.

"I'm already registered. I'll need a room for Miss Thorenson. Are you renting a room, Miss Blackburn?" he asked pointedly.

"I suppose," she replied, looking toward Maura.

"That's not necessary," Maura interjected. "She can stay in my room tonight."

"Why don't you freshen up and then we'll go to dinner—alone," he said.

"I'll need a little time," she replied, although not sure she would ever be ready to spend any time alone with such a dour man.

"I'll make arrangements for the trunks to be delivered to your room. Meet me here at five o'clock—without her," he responded.

"I understood she wasn't invited the first time you told me to come alone," she replied and walked away, feeling his eyes following her.

❧

"You look lovely. That dress was a wonderful choice," Georgette offered as Maura prepared to leave. The deep green bodice was embellished with gold trim, and the three deep pink flounces of the skirt were bordered with forest green edging. Her auburn hair fell in soft waves around her face, reaching below the neckline of her dress, while the remainder was pulled into a large bun surrounded by a matching green ribbon.

"Thank you, Georgette, but I don't think Mr. Buchanan will be overly impressed," she answered, picking up her long wool cape and placing it over her shrunken arm.

At exactly five o'clock she walked into the hotel foyer, where Luther was impatiently pacing back and forth. She was pleased to see that he wasn't wearing the same attire in which he'd met the ship. He wore gray wool trousers, a white shirt with gray cravat topped by a double-breasted waistcoat, and a black alpaca frock coat. He carried a black beaver felt top hat and his chestnut hair was cut short and parted on the side. A dark brown mustache showed a hint of gray, making him look older than his avowed age of thirty years. Although his face appeared permanently etched in a frown, he wasn't altogether unpleasant in his appearance.

"Have I kept you waiting long?" she asked as she approached him.

He pulled his watch from his waistcoat. "It doesn't matter how long I've been waiting. You are exactly on time. It's five o'clock," he replied.

Once again she felt as though his eyes were boring through her. The silence was deafening. "Are we dining here?" she inquired when he neither said anything further nor moved toward the door.

"No," he replied and extended his arm. "There's a restaurant a short distance away. I thought we could walk. That is, if you're able to walk that far?"

"You'd be surprised just how far I can walk, Mr. Buchanan," she said, wanting to add that if she weren't so far from home, she'd walk right out of his life. Instead, she held her tongue and took his arm.

Not another word passed between them until they were seated in the restaurant and Luther had ordered dinner for both of them.

"Now, then," he began, "how is it you failed to mention in your letters that you're a cripple—or didn't you think I'd notice?" he asked sarcastically.

"I was sure you would notice, Mr. Buchanan, unless you had a problem with your vision," Maura shot back, unable to hold her temper in check.

"Well, I don't have a problem seeing, and if I did, I would have told you. In fact, I would have told you if I suffered from any infirmity," he retaliated, his voice flooded with anger.

"Mr. Buchanan, I do not suffer from anything. I happen to have an arm and leg that are somewhat shriveled. My left leg causes me to limp, and I am somewhat limited in the use of my left hand and arm, but I do not consider myself a cripple— wasn't that the word you used—cripple?"

"It seems to me if you weren't afraid I'd have rejected you, you would have told me. You were careful to send a picture that hid your imperfection and just as careful not to write me about it. Is that why you've never married? No one would have you?"

Maura stared back at him for just a moment and then very quietly replied, "It's very likely that the reason I remain unmarried is because I have visible physical differences. You're right. I was afraid you would find me unacceptable because of that divergence from what the world considers normal. I'm sorry that I didn't tell you, because it's obvious you find me outwardly displeasing. Unfortunately, I must tell you that I find you even more unsuitable. You don't realize it, Luther, but you are much more crippled than I—inwardly crippled by a cruel spirit and vicious tongue. Now, if you'll excuse me, I've lost my appetite," she concluded, rising from the table.

"No, I won't excuse you. This matter needs to be settled, and walking out of here isn't going to resolve anything. Please, sit down," he appealed.

Realizing he was right and that they had to make some decisions, Maura sat down just as their dinner arrived. She watched as Luther began to eat, though she was unable to regain any desire for food.

"You need help cutting your meat?" he asked when he noticed she hadn't begun her dinner.

"No, I don't need help cutting my meat, combing my hair, or washing dishes, Luther. I lead a perfectly normal life, although I'm sure you find that hard to believe," she replied.

"I was just offering to help," he answered defensively.

"I think it would be best if I returned to Boston," Maura told him in an emotionless voice.

"Now hold up just a minute," Luther responded in between bites of mashed potatoes and gravy. "I think you're forgetting how much money I've already spent getting you here. Not to mention the fact that I've lost a whole year what with waiting the six months you requested and then almost six months for your voyage."

"As far as your capital outlay is concerned, I could send you monthly payments until you're reimbursed. There's nothing I can do to replace your time."

"You have money for your return voyage?" he inquired.

She met his eyes. "No, I don't. You'll have to advance it, and I'll repay that also," she said.

"Sorry, but I don't have that kind of money right now. I'm in San Francisco not only to meet your ship but also to purchase the supplies I ordered to restock my store. I don't have an extra thousand dollars to send you home. In fact, I don't think there are too many choices available to us. The preacher's already been paid and agreed to conduct the wedding tomorrow morning. I'll honor my word that we'll be married—in name only," he hastened to add, when she tried to interrupt him.

"Do I have any say in this?" she asked, unable to remain calm any longer.

"Not really. You don't have the money to return home; you don't have any family here; you can't support yourself; and even if you could, no self-respecting single woman would want to live alone and unprotected in San Francisco. The town is swarming with men—most of them with very little regard for a lady," he replied.

"In other words, I should be thankful that you're willing to sacrifice yourself and marry me?"

"Well, I wouldn't exactly put it in those words, but—"

"I'll say one thing for you, Mr. Buchanan. What you lack in character you certainly make up for in arrogance," she retorted.

"If you can think of another way to solve this, I'm all ears," he countered.

"If and when I do, you'll be the first to know. I'd like to return to the hotel now if you've finished your dinner."

They walked back to the hotel in a deafening silence. "I'll meet you here at ten o'clock in the morning. The preacher's expecting us at ten-thirty," Luther instructed as he pulled his watch from the pocket of his waistcoat.

"Counting up your hours of freedom?" Maura baited him, unable to restrain herself.

He didn't give a rejoinder but merely started down the hallway with Maura staring after him. She was startled when he abruptly turned and came back.

"Did you bring a wedding gown?" he asked.

"Yes," she responded, surprised by the question.

"Wear it," he commanded and once again walked away from her. "And you can bring that Blackburn woman along if you want," he called back over his shoulder, surprising her even further.

When he finally disappeared from sight and Maura was sure he wasn't returning, she left the foyer and returned to her room. Georgette was sitting in a large overstuffed chair that appeared to have her submerged in its depths.

"Wouldn't that other chair be more comfortable?" Maura inquired as she removed her cape.

"I think so and I would certainly like to try it, but I can't seem to get out of this one," Georgette replied. "Every time I attempt to stand up I'm thrown off balance and land right back where I started from. It seems my legs are too short and my belly is too large," she explained with a giggle. "I was beginning to fear I would have to spend the night in this chair. I don't know what I would have done if you hadn't returned," she added.

"Here, let me help you," Maura said, extending her good arm to the girl and watching as Georgette ungracefully made her way across the room and lowered herself into the smaller chair.

"Oh, this is much better. Now, tell me what happened at dinner," she encouraged.

Maura related only a portion of the events, not wanting to relive all of the painful exchanges that had transpired earlier in the evening.

"This is so exciting! Obviously, I'm not a good judge of people. When we met Mr. Buchanan on the dock he seemed so sullen that I was fearful he would be mean-spirited about— well, you know. . ." she said, her voice trailing off.

"You mean about my being a cripple?" Maura said for her.

"I never called you any such thing," Georgette flared in return.

"No, you didn't—that's what Luther Buchanan calls me," she said, unable to hold back the pain any longer. Until that moment she hadn't realized the wounds he had reopened. All the old sorrow from years gone by came rushing back to haunt her, and she was unable to hold back the racking sobs that spilled forth from deep within.

Georgette moved as quickly as her body would allow and embraced her friend, smoothing her hair and attempting somehow to relieve a small portion of Maura's agony.

"I am so very sorry, Maura. He can't even begin to imagine what a wonderful person you are. It will all work out. You'll see," she crooned.

As soon as the words were spoken, Georgette burst out with a cry of agony. "Oh, Maura, I think I've begun my labor," she sobbed, doubling over in her attempt to reach the bed.

# four

The next morning Luther doggedly paced back and forth in the lobby, pulling out his pocket watch every thirty seconds. It was almost eleven o'clock, but Maura hadn't appeared. He knew that he had told her they were to meet the preacher at eleven, and they were obviously going to be late. Fear slowly crept into his mind that perhaps she had fled during the night, deciding marriage to him was a worse fate than fending for herself in unknown territory. His thoughts raced back to the small church in Virginia where he had stood waiting for Elizabeth five years earlier.

"It's happened again," he murmured as he once again looked down at the timepiece.

Snapping the watch closed and returning it to the pocket of his embroidered blue satin waistcoat, which had been specially ordered for this occasion, he resolutely walked toward Maura's room and rapped loudly on the door. Several minutes had passed when, just as he raised his hand to knock once again, the door swung open.

Maura stood before him in the same dress she had been wearing when they had parted company last evening. It appeared wet in places and stained in others; her hair was damp, and the waves from the night before were straight and unkempt. Dark circles under her eyes made them appear sunken into her head, and her limp as she walked away from him seemed even more exaggerated than he remembered.

"Come in and close the door if you care to stay," she said, not looking back to see if he'd entered or not.

"Would you care to tell me what's going on?" he asked, slamming the door.

His answer came from the adjoining room—the lusty cry of a newborn who had struggled into the world only minutes before.

"I've been acting as Georgette's midwife all night. Obviously, I'll not be ready for a wedding at eleven o'clock," she stated, confirming the obvious.

"You mean we're going to be held up until tomorrow? I don't even know if the preacher is available then. How long will it take you to get ready? I can go and see if he'll wait another hour. Can you be ready by noon?" he asked, his questions fired in rapid succession.

Maura walked back and stood directly in front of him. "Luther, I just told you that I've been up all night. Look at me. Do I look like I can be ready for a wedding in less than an hour? As soon as things quiet down, I plan to clean up and then get some much-needed rest. So if you're determined to get married today, you'll have to find another bride," she answered, for the first time looking directly into his eyes.

"Well, can you give me some idea when you'll be able to find time to attend the wedding?" he inquired, running his hand through his thick brown hair while meeting her gaze.

"I'd prefer to wait for at least two weeks," she calmly replied.

"Two weeks!" he shouted. His protest was quickly followed by the robust cries of the infant.

"Would you please refrain from shouting and slamming doors? I'm sure that Georgette would appreciate it, and I know I certainly would," she said, annoyed that he had wakened the baby.

"My humble apologies, Miss Thorenson. It would be nice if you'd remember who is paying for these rooms. It isn't Miss Blackburn or her newborn. It would also be appreciated if you would remember just why you came to California!"

"I know who is paying the hotel bill, and I know why I came to California. How could I forget? But you see, Mr. Buchanan,

I would be failing miserably if I were to leave this girl alone with a newborn. She has no one. Who will help her? To be honest, I don't know if I'll be able to force myself to leave her in two weeks," she continued.

Luther fell into the large wing chair that had threatened to swallow Georgette only the night before. In contrast, he seemed to dwarf the overstuffed piece of furniture as he folded his hands together and leaned forward, resting his elbows on his knees.

"It seems as though we're once again going to be forced to make some difficult decisions," he commented.

"Obviously your idea of joint decision-making is different than mine. As I recall, there weren't any real choices to be made."

"Well, in that case, why don't you go first? Tell me your plan for resolving this situation. Believe me, I'd love to hear your solution."

Maura hadn't expected him to turn the tables, but now she was confronted with presenting a workable arrangement when her mind was barely functioning from lack of sleep. She seated herself across from him on the brocade settee.

"Why can't you just wait for several weeks before we leave for Placerville?" she asked, unable to offer anything further at the moment.

"Why? I'll tell you why. I own a store in Placerville that is being operated by a man who is more interested in returning to the gold fields than taking care of my business. When I left, I was sorely in need of supplies, and I've already been gone three weeks what with my travel time and waiting for the supplies and your ship to arrive. I was expecting to be back before now, and you want me to remain here several more weeks? Time is money! I have a schedule to keep. For some insane reason, I thought having a wife was going to help me run my store more efficiently. If I listen to you, I won't have a business left to run!"

"Is that what I'm to be, then? Someone to act as your hired help in the mercantile?" she challenged.

"Let's not even get into that," he replied angrily. "We're supposed to be looking for a solution, not finding additional problems to argue over. If you have any other ideas, this is your chance to air them, because it is out of the question for us to remain here," he said, giving her one more opportunity to solve the matter.

"If the preacher is available to marry us tomorrow, we can leave shortly after the ceremony. Before we depart, you'll need to make a bed in the back of the wagon for Georgette and the baby," she answered.

"What?" he bellowed, jumping from the chair. "You think I should take that woman and her baby with us to Placerville? Are you planning on them living with us, too? I can't believe this," he continued ranting as he paced back and forth in the small sitting room.

"You want to return immediately, and I can't leave her here alone. It's going to be difficult for her to make the trip so soon after the baby's birth, but I think she'll agree."

"You think she'll agree? You think she'll agree? Well, of course she'll agree. Why shouldn't she? All of a sudden she has an instant family to take care of her. If it isn't being too inquisitive, might I ask just what this woman had in mind when she set sail for California in her condition? Or is she totally mindless?"

"Keep your voice down. She doesn't need to hear your caustic remarks; it's quite enough that I must tolerate them. She's young and made a mistake. Her family disowned her, and her father's final gift to her was passage on the *Edward Everett* with the admonition never to contact the family again. Someone told her that men greatly outnumbered women in California, so I suppose her plan was that she would find a husband after the baby was born."

"If, and I'm just saying if, I agree to take her with us, what then? Do you plan on her living with us? Because I'll not agree to that," he weakly replied.

*He knows I can't agree to that,* Maura thought. *I can see it in his eyes.* Aloud she gave him the answer she knew he expected. "She'll have to stay until she's able to make other arrangements."

He slowly shook his head. "Maura, you know I've got to return and I'm bound to my pledge to marry you. I'll take them with us and they can stay for two months. If she has any money, I expect her to pay for her board. I want your promise that at the end of two months, Miss Blackburn and her child will move from our home—with no excuses, no extensions, and no argument from you. Do we have a deal?"

Maura thought for only a moment. "You have my word. After you've talked with the preacher, let me know when I'm to be prepared for the marriage ceremony. I'll be on time," she added.

"I'll not come back until dinner time so that you can rest. Hopefully, I'll have finalized the arrangements by then," he replied, once again removing his pocket watch, checking the time, and returning it to his waistcoat.

Once he'd left, Maura leaned against the closed door, unable to believe that he had agreed to her terms but too tired to delight in the victory. She tiptoed into the bedroom, where Georgette and the baby were sleeping. Quietly she poured water into the china washbowl and bathed herself and, even though it was past noon, slipped into a soft cotton nightgown.

Several hours later, the baby's vigorous cries and Georgette's voice pulled her out of a deep sleep.

"What time is it?" she called out from the sitting room, her back aching from sleeping on the small settee.

"I don't know," Georgette called back, "but I'm getting terribly hungry. Is there anything here to eat?"

"No, but I'll get you something as soon as I get dressed," Maura assured her as she walked into the bedroom.

Certain that it must be close to five o'clock, she pulled a pale blue silk dress with navy piping and a lace collar from her trunk. Moving quickly, she brushed her hair and pulled it into a chignon at the back of her head. Somewhere in her trunk were blue ribbons that matched the dress, but in her haste she was unable to find them. Giving up, she pulled out her silk bonnet just as a knock sounded at the door.

Luther greeted her while holding a covered plate of food and pot of steaming tea he had carried over from the restaurant. "I thought Miss Blackburn would be hungry," he stated, extending the plate toward her as he walked in the door.

"Thank you, Luther. I know Georgette will be most appreciative," she said, caught off guard by his thoughtful gesture.

"I just didn't want you rushing me through dinner so that you could get her meal back here. I knew that was what would happen," he replied.

*Now, that's more in his character,* Maura thought. *What I momentarily mistook for kindness is not kindness at all— merely a continuation of his self-serving attitude.*

She took the platter to Georgette and waited until the new mother was settled with her dinner before returning to the sitting room. Luther was pacing back and forth, obviously irritated at having to wait an extra few minutes. Maura was tempted to tell him that she needed to change the baby's diaper before they could leave but then thought better of purposefully irritating him.

The restaurant wasn't crowded when they arrived, and Maura requested that they be seated near one of the windows.

"Being able to look outdoors while you're dining is nice, don't you think?" she ventured in an attempt to have a civil conversation while they ate dinner.

"Personally, I don't like people watching me eat," he replied.

"So much for civil conversation," she murmured under her breath.

"Excuse me? I didn't hear you," he answered.

"Oh, nothing. Were you able to find the preacher?" she asked, intentionally changing the subject.

"Yes, and I might add that he wasn't very happy. Apparently he sat around for several hours waiting on us. He said he'd meet us at the church at eleven o'clock tomorrow and not a minute later. Of course, he expected extra compensation for his inconvenience," Luther was quick to inform her.

"Of course," she answered.

He waited, but when she said nothing further, he leaned forward in his chair. "You will be ready on time, won't you?"

"Yes, Luther, I'll be ready on time. You will have the wagon prepared for Georgette and the baby, won't you?" she rebutted.

"I've already seen to it," he smugly retorted.

*Why is it I allow him to make me so irritable?* Maura thought. *It seems as though he takes pleasure in making me angry. How can I spend the rest of my life with this cantankerous man?*

"The supplies are already loaded, so we'll be able to leave shortly after the ceremony. We'll be taking three wagons," he said, jolting her back to the present.

"Three wagons? How can we do that?" she inquired.

"I've hired a couple of men. It's got nothing to do with you and Miss Blackburn. I always need at least three wagons to get my supplies back to Placerville," he added.

"Well, it's good to know that at least one thing isn't our fault," she replied, but then was sorry for not holding her tongue.

❧

Morning arrived all too soon, and Maura carefully prepared herself. She had slipped into her chemise when Georgette offered to lace her corset, explaining that she could easily perform the task without leaving the confines of her bed.

"You don't even need this corset. I believe your waist is just as small without it," Georgette dolefully remarked while looking at her own figure.

"Don't worry, Georgette. You'll be back to a tiny waistline in no time," Maura replied, beginning to run the brush through her hair.

"Let me do your hair," Georgette requested. "I'd like to do something for you after all you've done for me," she continued when Maura didn't immediately move toward her.

Maura smiled and handed her the hairbrush. "Let me pull the chair close to the bed so that you can manage."

Patiently Georgette fashioned the thick auburn hair into long, plump curls that would accentuate Maura's coronet headpiece of crystal-beaded flowers and waxed orange blossoms, which held her three-quarter-length veil. "There!" she proudly announced when she had finished. "It looks beautiful."

Knowing she dared not be late, Maura checked the time and carefully stepped into the silk wedding gown. Ivory silk lace edged the pleated bertha, and the gusseted bodice formed an exaggerated V-shape just below her waist. The long sleeves were accented with the same ivory lace that surrounded the bertha. The dome-shaped skirt was held in place by whale-bone hoops, which were sewn into her petticoats, and her white lisle stockings were embroidered with blond lace. She slipped on a pair of low-heeled ivory shoes decorated with tiny lace bows. She carried a small bouquet fashioned from ribbons, lace, and waxed orange blossoms and leaves that matched her headpiece.

"Oh, Maura, you look gorgeous. You even thought to make a bouquet before leaving home."

"Actually, my mother made it," she replied while digging deeper into one of her trunks. "I can't seem to find my hand-kerchief or netted mitts."

"May I help you look?" Georgette inquired.

"Don't you dare get out of that bed," Maura retorted, pulling a silk reticule from the depths of the trunk. "Oh, look—my mitts and handkerchief are inside," she said, finally feeling a sense of relief.

She took a fleeting look into the mirror. "This certainly isn't the wedding I imagined when mother and I were spending hours choosing fabric and lace. But I suppose it really doesn't matter," she commented.

"Of course it matters," Georgette told her. "You get married only once, and you're a beautiful bride. I just wish I could be there," her friend lamented.

"I may be a bride, but it doesn't appear I'll ever be a wife or mother. This whole thing is a mockery, and if I had any sense at all, I'd tell Luther Buchanan that I'm not willing to settle for half a marriage. Please don't waste your time wishing you could observe this travesty. I'd better leave. Mr. Buchanan is quite a stickler for being on time," she said, leaning down to place a kiss on the baby girl's soft cheek.

"I've decided to name her Rachel Rebecca Blackburn. I named her after you and Rachel. I thought we could call her Becca," Georgette said, her eyes filling with tears. "You can't begin to imagine how much I appreciate all you've done for me. How will I ever repay you?"

"You named your baby after me, and I'll have the pleasure of being with the two of you a while longer. How could I ask for anything more? I think that Rachel Rebecca Blackburn is a beautiful name, and I know Rachel would be pleased as punch to have this beautiful child as her namesake. Now, get some rest and enjoy the comfort of that bed while you can. Soon you'll be riding in a wagon and won't think I've done you such a favor. I'll be back in an hour or so," she said, walking toward the door and holding the bouquet in her withered left hand.

As expected, Luther was pacing back and forth through the foyer when she arrived. He looked up as she approached him at the end of the hallway.

"You look. . ."

"I look what?" she asked when he didn't complete the sentence.

"Oh, nothing. Hurry or we'll be late. There's a carriage

outside. I thought we would look odd walking down the street in our wedding attire," he told her, moving toward the front door.

"My, don't you make a beautiful bride," the owner of the hotel said as he held the front door open for the couple.

"Thank you, sir," she answered.

Luther made no comment, but she noticed that his face and neck reddened at the man's flattering remark. *Either he doesn't think I look nice enough to receive a compliment, or he's embarrassed since he failed to mention my appearance,* Maura thought.

It was a brief and unremarkable ceremony, each of them pledging to honor and obey the other, followed by the minister pronouncing them man and wife. Maura noticed the preacher's perplexed look when Luther didn't take advantage of his announcement that he could now "kiss the new bride."

Enjoying his apparent embarrassment, Maura couldn't resist making the situation even more difficult for him.

"Luther," she sweetly implored, "didn't you hear the minister say that you could kiss me?" she asked, her eyelashes fluttering as she looked from the preacher back toward Luther, hoping he would feel an iota of the humiliation she was bearing due to his oafish attitude.

"I'm sorry. A kiss—is that what you're wanting?" he asked, the anger in his eyes directed at his new bride.

Immediately she knew she'd gone too far and had just opened her mouth to apologize when she felt her body being crushed against his. The fullness of his lips covered hers with a reckless intensity that left her breathless. Leaning into him, she felt a passion rise inside that she had never known existed. Her whole body felt weak, and her knees threatened to buckle at any moment. Without thought, she placed her hand around the nape of his neck, pulling his head toward her, never wanting the moment to end.

Reaching back and removing her hand, Luther shifted away

from her. "I believe one kiss was the requirement," he coldly remarked.

Maura felt the blood rush to her face and wanted to run from the church—as far away from his cruel remark as her legs would carry her. *Seeing me run would really give him cause for laughter,* she thought, wishing she could quell the fury and outrage rising inside her.

With a modicum of dignity remaining, Maura turned and quietly limped toward the doors of the church. *This is my husband, 'til death do us part. Lord, when will I ever learn to control my tongue,* she half-thought and half-prayed, knowing it would be better had she never experienced the wonder of that impassioned kiss.

## *five*

Standing behind the counter of the Buchanan Mercantile Store, Luther watched as Maura laboriously measured and cut fabric for one of the few women who lived at the diggings with her husband. The customer probably hadn't seen another woman for six months, and her mouth had begun moving the minute she eyed Maura and still hadn't stopped. He noticed Maura giving the woman a smile every now and then or nodding her head, but the stranger didn't seem to want conversation, merely a set of female ears to hear all the unspoken thoughts she had stored up in the past six or eight months.

Maura led the woman through the store while pointing out or suggesting different items, all of which the customer agreed to purchase. Walking toward the counter, Maura looked toward Luther.

"Have you sold all of the Christmas nutcrackers?" she asked, looking at the shelf behind him and seeing only an empty space.

"I'm afraid so. I didn't expect they'd be so popular, or I'd have ordered more," he replied. "They were all sold just a few days after Thanksgiving."

The woman's face dropped in obvious disappointment at the announcement. "I've been saving a little money each week to buy one," she related. "I saw some last Christmas when we came to town, and I've been wanting one ever since."

Maura had been listening to the woman talk for almost an hour. It was obvious that she had come searching for a better life and was hungry for an existence beyond the gold diggings. It seemed so pitiful. *Not so much different from my circumstances,* Maura thought. *I came searching for a life beyond*

*what I had, and I've settled for being a wife in name only—
while giving my time to work in this store, in addition to caring
for the house and tending to his needs.*

"I'll be back in just a minute. Please don't leave," Maura
told the woman. "You'll need to figure up her bill, Luther," she
called over her shoulder and left the store with both of them
gazing after her.

"I want you to take this and enjoy it," Maura told the woman
a short time later. The woman was outside loading their wagon
with her purchases while Luther was helping her husband carry
out some of the heavier provisions from the back of the store.

"Oh, I can't take this," the woman said, pulling back the
brown paper.

"Of course, you can. I want you to have it. Believe me, it
will give me far greater pleasure in your possession than in
mine," Maura convincingly replied.

"If you really insist," the woman answered in a faltering
voice. Without hesitation, she wrapped her arms around
Maura. "Thank you, thank you so much. I don't remember the
last time someone did something for me, not expecting anything in return. God love ya," she whispered, a tear rolling
down her cheek as she released Maura from her embrace.

"Look, Jed! Look what she gave me," the woman excitedly
called to her husband as he and Luther reached the wagon.

Maura didn't look toward Luther as the woman proudly dis-
played the brightly painted nutcracker. "Ain't it just grand?"

"That it is, that it is. I'm not sure why you think having one
of those things is so important, but I gotta admit it's good to
see you smile," he told her. "Thank you for your kindness,
ma'am," he said, tipping his hat toward Maura.

"You're quite welcome. It was my pleasure," she said,
embarrassed by their zealous expressions of thankfulness. "I'd
better get inside. Have a safe journey."

"Thanks again, and Merry Christmas!" the woman called
after her.

Maura stopped short upon hearing the wish for a merry Christmas. Soon it would be Christmas—the deadline for Georgette and Becca to move from Luther's house. Merry Christmas no longer seemed like a joyous greeting but, instead, a quickly approaching ultimatum.

Maura didn't turn back but merely waved her hand in recognition of the words that the woman had spoken. She had just gone to rearrange the shelf of fabrics when she felt Luther's breath on the back of her neck.

"Would you like to tell me why you gave that stranger my nutcracker?" he asked in a steady voice.

"I didn't realize it was your nutcracker. You brought it home shortly after I arrived, and as I recall, you said something to the effect that I might find it either useful or decorative during the holidays," she answered.

"That's right. But I didn't mean it was yours to give away. I meant exactly what I said—that it might be useful as a decoration and to crack nuts during the holidays."

"Since I find nutcrackers rather unattractive, I wouldn't want to use one as a decoration, and utilizing one to crack nuts is more for novelty than quick results. I'm sorry we've once again misunderstood each other. It seems that's what we do best," she commented as she began to straighten another shelf of goods.

"Those nutcrackers aren't cheap, you know. And you just gave it to her—a complete stranger," he said, following after her.

"Consider it payment for the privilege of working in your store," she retaliated.

"Working? You think the little bit you accomplish around here is work? As slow as you move, it's about the same as having no help at all. It took you twice as long to measure and cut that material as it would a normal woman," he fired back.

"Normal woman? First I'm a cripple, and now I'm abnormal. Well, Luther, I'm going to take my crippled, abnormal body out of your store. Since I'm of little assistance, it's good to know I won't be causing you any great loss," she said, limping toward the door, tears beginning to form in her eyes as she slammed the door behind her.

"Maura! Wait up a minute. . ." Luther called from the doorway.

She heard him but didn't stop walking.

"Maura!" he hollered. "Since you're going home, why don't you empty those extra trunks so that I can get them out of the house. There's always folks needing steamer trunks. Most likely I'll be able to sell them in short order."

She stopped in her tracks. *Silly woman! He wasn't calling after you to apologize. All he wanted was to be sure that you didn't go home and rest or enjoy yourself for a few minutes,* she thought and once again picked up her pace without acknowledging his comment.

Entering the house quietly, she was careful not to disturb Georgette or Becca. She knew that Georgette would question her about why she was home in the middle of the day, and the last thing she wanted to do was answer questions. Although Georgette was aware of Luther's attitude before the wedding, Maura believed it was improper to discuss their ongoing problems now that they were man and wife. When all of them were together, both Maura and Luther remained civil with each other, and Georgette was left to assume the two had resolved their earlier problems. Although it was obvious they weren't ecstatically in love, they appeared to be adjusting to married life—at least to everyone else.

Hanging her coat on the peg inside their bedroom door, Maura's eyes fell upon Rachel's trunks. Except for dusting, she hadn't touched them since Luther placed them along the west wall of the room upon their arrival. Pulling the wooden rocker from the corner, she sat down and unlatched the largest trunk. Methodically, she began inspecting the items, although feeling like an uninvited intruder into Rachel's life. When she had

completed the task, she sat surrounded by stacks of belongings—those she would keep, those Georgette might want, and
those that could be given to the needy. The stack to be given
away was by far the largest, since Rachel's clothing was styled
for a woman of differing proportions and age than Maura or
Georgette. Just as Maura was completing the chore, Georgette
walked into the room carrying Becca.

"I thought I heard someone in here. What are you doing?"
Georgette inquired.

"Luther thought I should go through Rachel's belongings so
that he could move the trunks out of the bedroom," she
answered. "I've picked out some items that may appeal to you.
Why don't you look at them, and if you're not interested, I'll
put them in that stack," Maura instructed, pointing toward the
pile to be given away.

"Don't you want any of this?" Georgette asked, beginning to
pick through the jewelry.

"I've already looked at it and I did choose this one pin as a
remembrance, but if you like it, I'll take another. I've also kept
her journal. She has a lovely Bible, Georgette. I'd like you to
take it. That way you'd have your own for our daily Bible
readings and for church services. Rachel had marked so many
wonderful passages and made little notes along the margins. I
think it will become a real blessing to you as you explore
God's word," Maura tentatively suggested.

"I'd be honored," Georgette replied, opening the pages and
looking at the underlined scriptures.

Shortly after they had met on the ship, Rachel had suggested
the three of them join together for a daily Bible study.
Embarrassed by her lack of spiritual training, Georgette had
confided in Maura that her father did not believe in God. Even
worse, he had forbidden any members of the family to attend
church or study the Bible. It was the one rule all of them had
kept.

It hadn't been an easy task convincing Georgette that Rachel would view her lack of religious training as a challenge presented by God himself. Maura had carefully explained that Rachel would find it a privilege to introduce Georgette to the Lord. And she had. Before her untimely accident, Rachel had spent many hours nurturing, explaining, and guiding Georgette in God's Word. Through Rachel's loving spirit and God-given patience, she had led Georgette down the path of salvation.

It had been a wonderful experience for Maura to observe the changes that continued to take place in Georgette's life since her introduction to God's grace and love. Precisely in God's timing, she seemed to grow in her newfound faith. Much as Becca was thriving in her mother's love and adoration, Georgette was flourishing in God's loving acceptance of her as one of His children.

"Are you thinking about our Bible studies with Rachel?" Georgette asked, pulling Maura from her thoughts.

"Yes. She was such a fine lady and I miss her. It was such a privilege to meet her, but I'm sure the Lord is showering her with rewards as we speak," Maura answered, giving Georgette a smile.

"Do you think she would have forgiven me for having a child out of wedlock? I wish now I would have told her, but I was afraid she wouldn't want to associate with me."

"She would have forgiven you, Georgette, and she would have told you that if you seek God's forgiveness, it is there for the taking. Do you remember how excited Rachel was when you accepted Jesus?"

Georgette nodded her head.

"Being an unwed mother wouldn't have changed any of that. Jesus knew you were going to have a child, but He didn't turn you away. Surely you know in your heart that Rachel would have done no less."

"You're right. She would have been loving and supportive, just like you. I guess it was easier to talk to you since you're younger."

"Perhaps, but if you recall, you didn't tell me, either. I only found out because of your illness. I don't think you were all that trusting of me, either," Maura answered with a laugh. "I'd better finish up before Luther gets home. Do you feel good enough to sit at the table and peel some potatoes?"

"Of course I do. You go ahead and finish up in here. I'll put Becca back in her cradle and have those potatoes ready in no time," she replied.

Going through all of Rachel's belongings had been more of a chore than she'd expected. She lifted the lid of the remaining trunk, pleased it was the smallest. Primarily it appeared to contain Rachel's family mementos and knickknacks. Picking up what appeared to be an old leather reticule, Maura was surprised at its weight when she attempted to pull it toward her. Carefully, she untied the leather thongs holding it tightly closed.

"Georgette! Come here, right now!" she called out, forgetting the sleeping baby.

"What is it? What's wrong?" Georgette asked, rushing into the room.

"Look," she said, holding the leather bag open for her friend to see.

"Oh, Maura! I wonder how Rachel came by all that money," Georgette exclaimed.

"She told me she had sold just about everything she owned. She must have owned quite a bit from the looks of what's in this bag."

"What are you going to do with it?" Georgette asked.

"I'm not sure. She had no family left, so I guess it's ours. We'll split it. You can do what you want with your half, and I'll do what I want with mine," Maura suggested.

"It's not half mine. The captain gave the trunks to you—it's yours," Georgette insisted, sounding frightened by the discovery.

"Georgette," Maura said, exasperated with the girl's

demeanor, "we didn't steal this. There's nothing to be afraid of." Hearing Luther's footsteps on the wooden porch, she whispered, "Please don't say anything about this in front of Luther, at least not just yet."

"Whatever you say," Georgette agreed, watching Maura place the bag in the carved oak chiffonier and then cover it with several articles of clothing.

"Where's supper?" Luther asked, walking into the bedroom just as Maura returned to the rocking chair. Georgette quickly exited.

"I thought you wanted me to clean out these trunks," she replied. "I realize a normal person could have finished by now, but as you can see—"

"Stop it!" he ordered. "You've made it abundantly clear that I hurt your feelings. In fact, you always make it abundantly clear when you're unhappy. Which, I might add, is most of the time. I told you the first time I laid eyes on you that I needed a wife to help in the store—someone that could keep up at a regular pace. I'm aware that you try, but there is no way you're ever going to be able to perform as much or as quickly as someone without your. . ."

He hesitated, apparently knowing whatever word he used would be wrong.

Maura didn't fill in the word for him. "Luther, if I don't meet your needs in the store, perhaps you should hire someone."

"I've been thinking along those lines," he quickly replied.

"You have?" Maura asked, startled by his answer.

"Let's go out to the kitchen," he suggested.

Georgette was busy mixing cornbread when the two of them entered the kitchen.

"I'll be done with this in just a minute and then I'll be out of your way," she said, seeming to sense something was amiss.

"No, sit down," Luther offered, in an unusually benevolent manner.

Looking toward Maura for confirmation, Georgette seated

herself when she saw her friend nod.

"Maura and I have been talking about how difficult it is for her to meet my expectations as a wife. In helping at the store, that is," he quickly added when both of the women's heads simultaneously jerked up and their mouths dropped open.

"I meant, you know, with her. . .ailment, it's uh. . .harder for her than a. . ." he stammered, looking for the right words.

A deafening silence followed, neither of the women saying a word.

"What I'm trying to say is that you've been living here with us, Georgette, and although you haven't said anything to me outright, I'm sure you've been feeling you owe us something for all we've done for you and your baby."

"Luther! How dare you say such a rude thing to Georgette! I thought you wanted to talk about hiring someone to work at the store." Just as she had uttered her last word, the realization hit her like a bolt of lightning. "Oh—I see, I see," she said, beginning to rise from her chair while Georgette unwittingly viewed the unfolding scene, her eyes darting back and forth between the two of them.

"Sit down, Maura," Luther commanded, his voice leaving no doubt she should be seated. "I'm not proposing anything illegal or immoral, so you best just settle down." He paused momentarily and looked at Georgette. "I feel it would be well within your Christian duty, Georgette, to repay us for our kindness by working at the store for a period of time. That way Maura could take care of the house and care for Becca while you're working. It would be much easier on Maura, and I'm sure you'd prefer to make life easier for her. You see, it's not what you expected at all, is it?" Luther asked Maura when he'd finished his proposal.

"It's exactly what I expected! I've learned what's most important to you in the short time we've been married, and it's not a wife. What you want is free labor to work in your store, and Georgette is a perfect slave. Just use a little guilt and feeling of obligation and she'll come running to work for you. Tell me, Luther, how do you sleep at night?" she asked, breaking her resolve to hide their marital discord from Georgette.

"Don't make me out to be the villain. If you'd been honest with me in the beginning, none of this would have happened," Luther shot back.

"You're right, Luther. What I did was misleading and dishonest, and if I had it to do over again, I'd certainly change things. But before there are any decisions made, I think we all three need to think and pray on this. It's not a decision that should be made in haste," she said, her voice quiet and subdued, a stark contrast to her earlier diatribe.

"I don't know what to say," Georgette remarked and rushed from the room.

❧

Maura hadn't returned to work in the store since the evening that Luther suggested Georgette replace her. During the days that followed, she and Georgette had spent much time in prayer, but only one answer had come to them. Although Maura had doubts, she had stepped out in faith that this answer was what God intended.

"I'm going to talk to Luther tonight, Georgette," Maura told her friend. "He's insisting upon an answer, and we're as ready as we can be under the circumstances."

"If you're sure. I don't want God holding me accountable for anything that's not in His will."

"I'm the one who will be held accountable for my own actions, Georgette. You haven't influenced me, and I truly believe that God's hand is at work in this. After dinner, why don't you take Becca into your bedroom while I talk to Luther in the kitchen."

However, Luther strode in the front door before Georgette had an opportunity to reply. As had become the custom over the past two weeks, after grace had been said, the only conversation at the dinner table was the little that was absolutely required to get through the meal.

Georgette rapidly downed her food and gulped a glass of milk as she rose from the table. "Sorry to rush off, but I need to check on Becca," she explained to no one in particular as she hurried from the room.

"She sure seems skittish tonight," Luther commented.

"We need to talk," Maura said, ignoring his remark about Georgette's behavior.

"Good, it's about time. Why don't you pour me another cup of coffee, and I'll have a big slice of that apple pie while we talk," he said, eyeing the buttery crust and tart apples.

Maura complied with his requests and then seated herself across from him. "I think you'd agree that this is not the marriage either of us intended," she began.

"Don't even start with that. . .I don't hold with divorce, and I'll not be hearing that kind of talk. Is that the solution you've come up with after two weeks of praying?"

"No, it isn't. As I said, this isn't the marriage either of us intended, and I don't think it's what God intended for us. I've prayed steadfastly for an answer and believe I've received one. I don't intend ever to speak of divorce, Luther, but I believe it would be best if we separated for a time. What I plan to do is move out of your house, but I'll remain here in town. I'm hopeful that one day soon we will be able to resolve our differences and begin our married life anew. Until then, I expect nothing from you and will take only the belongings I brought with me from Boston. I'll be leaving tomorrow, and, of course, Georgette and Becca will be moving at the same time."

He sat looking at her as though she hadn't spoken. After what seemed an eternity, he lifted his cup and took a drink of coffee. Carefully placing the cup on the table, he looked directly into her eyes.

"Just how do you and Georgette plan on supporting yourselves and Becca? Or am I allowed to ask?"

"We'll be just fine, Luther. I'm much more capable than you

think, but be assured that I truly want to make our marriage work. I just don't think it's possible right now."

"You avoided answering my question, so I guess that means it's none of my business. What if I told you I forbid you to leave—that you are my wife and you'll do as I say?" he asked.

"If you went so far as to say that, most likely I would stay. But you're not going to forbid me, are you, Luther?" she asked, already knowing the answer.

"No, I'm not going to forbid you. In fact, I'm not even going to ask you to stay. But when you've had your fill of trying to make it on your own, you need not ask permission to move back in. The house will be here, I'll be here, and your place will always remain here."

"Why, Luther?" she asked, in a strangled voice, the lump in her throat growing larger with each passing moment.

"I committed myself to this marriage. You're my wife, and your place is with me."

"Thank you for your honesty," she replied as an overwhelming sadness filled her being. His proclamation revealed what she already knew in her heart. The marriage was a contractual bargain he must fulfill—not out of his love and affection for her, but out of duty to God's word.

## six

The morning dawned crisp and cool with large puffy clouds lazily floating across a clear blue sky. Luther had been gone only a short time when a wagon pulled by two large draft horses drew in front of the house. Two men from the church loaded the trunks and belongings of the women and then urged the horses forward with a familiar "Giddyup."

Their destination was a house previously owned by Frank Millard, a banker who had become ill and died a short time after his arrival in Placerville. Maura had been told that his family moved back East and the house had remained vacant for almost six months. But now it belonged to Georgette and Maura, thanks to a measure of the money found in Rachel's trunk.

The women had spent a goodly portion of their time during the past week cleaning the house and preparing a list of necessities. It had been exciting, and Maura had been surprised that Luther hadn't gotten wind of their activities.

"There you are, ladies," one of the men announced while placing a trunk in the east bedroom. "That's the last of it. Looks a little sparse, but it won't take long before you'll have everything you need," he assured them.

"I'm sure we'll manage just fine for now, but we'll be glad when you've completed the rest of our furniture," Maura replied.

Michael Blanchard was an excellent carpenter and furniture maker. Georgette had approached him after church last Sunday with their order, and he had worked feverishly to complete several of the items. Rather sheepishly, he'd offered to loan them some of his own furniture in exchange for home-cooked meals. Maura suspected the handsome young man was more than a little interested in Georgette, although she seemed oblivious to his overtures.

"Well, what do you think?" Georgette asked as the two of them sat down to dinner in their new home.

"I think it's going to be fine," Maura replied, not wanting Georgette to know that she missed Luther's presence at the table.

"Do you really think we can be ready to open by the first of the year?" Georgette inquired when Maura added nothing further to the dinner conversation.

"What? Oh yes, at least the restaurant. If Michael can complete all the tables and chairs, we can sew the curtains and tablecloths. It won't matter that the serving dishes don't match. Most of our customers will be single men who care about the quality and quantity of their food, not whether their dinnerware matches that of everyone else in the room," she replied, smiling at the thought.

"It's almost too exciting to believe. I'm half owner of a business," Georgette said aloud as if to confirm the fact.

"It won't seem so difficult to believe when we're cooking, washing dishes, and waiting tables," Maura reminded her. "I think it's probably a good thing we won't be opening the rooming house part of our business until later," she added.

"Maybe it won't seem so overwhelming by taking on one boarder at a time. Michael said he'd finish the furniture for the bedrooms one by one, instead of doing all the beds and then all the washstands. He mentioned we might be taking on too much, but I don't think he was looking forward to making ten beds before moving along to something else," Georgette related.

"I'm sure he prefers a little variety in his work," Maura commented. "Sounds like the two of you have been chatting a good deal lately."

"Only about business," Georgette replied defensively.

"I was only teasing, Georgette. Besides, Michael is a fine young man who seems to be devout in his Christian beliefs. Furthermore, he's a hard worker, and I certainly admire his ability to withstand the gold fever that plagues the majority of the people in this area."

"He is a nice man, but I've had enough experience with men for now. Besides, I think Becca and our business will be more than enough to keep me occupied," Georgette replied.

Later that afternoon Maura left the house and began walking the short distance to Luther's store. They needed the fabric to begin making tablecloths and curtains for the restaurant, and Georgette had made it abundantly clear she didn't want to make the decision. Maura hadn't seen Luther since she had moved from his house, and she could feel her apprehension rising as she neared the store. The wind caught her woolen cloak, allowing a gust of cold air to thoroughly chill her entire being. Grasping at the flap, she pulled it back around her and pushed open the front door. The familiar tinkling of the bell and the warmth from the stove seemed almost welcoming as she entered and, except for two men who were inspecting the supplies, the store appeared empty.

Removing her cape and hanging it on the peg, she moved toward the yard goods and automatically began straightening the shelves.

"Excuse me, ma'am, but could you possibly help us? The owner said he'd be back shortly, but he's helping someone out in back."

"I can try," Maura replied. "What is it you're looking for?"

"We've just arrived and need to purchase supplies before we go to find our gold," one of them answered, seemingly assured there was gold patiently awaiting his arrival. "Placerville appears to be a quiet little town. I heard this place used to be called Hangtown. Is that true?"

"I haven't been here long myself, but unfortunately that story is true. I believe it was originally called Dry Diggings, but my husband told me that in 1849 three men were caught red-handed attempting to rob and murder a gold rusher nearby. It seems most of the miners were drunk and a kind of vigilante attitude overtook the mob. When someone asked the crowd what should be done with the three perpetrators, the crowd yelled, 'Hang them!' It turned into a chant and shortly thereafter the three men were stood in a wagon that had been placed under a tree to which three ropes had been attached. The men begged for mercy, for none was forthcoming. They were all hanged and it was because of that incident the town became known as Hangtown. Just last year, in 1851, the town was renamed Placerville," she told them as they followed her throughout the store while she selected items for them.

"Someone told me they serve something called 'Hangtown Fry' around here. What's that?" the other man inquired.

Maura smiled, recalling that she and Georgette had decided they wouldn't put "Hangtown Fry" on their menu when the restaurant opened. However, when Michael Blanchard overheard their discussion, he'd told them it was a mistake.

"People come here for the first time and they want to try 'Hangtown Fry.' You'll be making a mistake if you don't offer it. At least put it on the menu and if you see I'm wrong, you can always remove it," Michael had said, convincing both of them he was giving sound advice.

"Do you know what it is?" the other man asked when she hadn't immediately answered.

"Oh, yes. It's a fried mixture of oysters, eggs, and bacon," she replied.

"Is there a story behind that, too?" the first man inquired.

"Yes," she smiled. "It appears there's a story behind most things around here. Would you like to hear it?"

"Sure," one of them answered.

"It seems there was a hungry miner who had struck gold and came to town fresh from his claim and went to the hotel. Apparently he was feeling quite prosperous and asked for the most expensive meal the cook could prepare. He was told the most expensive item was oysters, followed by eggs. After thinking for a moment, he told the waiter to fry a mess of both and throw in some bacon. It's been a popular dish in these parts ever since," she related.

"We'll have to try some of that after we strike it rich," one of them said to Maura.

"You be sure and do that. I think I've gathered most of the items you'll need. Are you going to share a pan and rocker? They're rather expensive," she added, seeing their indecisiveness.

"I guess we'll just take one to start. What else have you put together for us?"

"You'll need beans, pork and bully beef, coffee, pick and shovel, bucket, frying pan and eating utensils. Do you have knives and sidearms?"

Both of them nodded affirmatively to that question.

"I don't know if you'll be interested in chewing tobacco, whiskey, or playing cards. A lot of the men request those items, although I'd advise against all of them," she added.

Before they'd had an opportunity to answer, Luther walked in the back door. "Sorry to keep you waiting so long, gentlemen," he apologized before catching a glimpse of Maura.

"We've been doing just fine. Your wife has kept us entertained while gathering our supplies," one of them answered.

"I'll let you finish up, Luther. I wanted to check some of the fabric for tablecloths and curtains," she explained, not wanting to say anything further in front of the strangers.

"Let's see what you've got here," Luther said to the men after nodding at Maura. "Appears she's just about got you outfitted. Will you be needing any weapons, ammunition, or whiskey?" he inquired, seeing none of those items in the accumulation.

"Don't think we'd better be spending what little money we've got left on whiskey, but I'd like a pouch of chewing tobacco and some playing cards," one of the men replied.

Once Luther and the men had loaded all of the supplies into the wagon, they returned to the store. Maura was measuring and cutting the fabric she'd decided upon. Although she could feel Luther's eyes on her as he calculated the men's purchases, neither of them said a word.

"Thanks for your help, ma'am," one of them called out to Maura.

"And for the fine storytelling, too," the other added.

"You're more than welcome. Best of luck to both of you. Stop by again when you need supplies," she answered, giving them a wide smile.

Maura had just completed folding the last piece of material when Luther returned.

"I really appreciate your help with those customers," Luther told her, a hint of warmth in his voice.

"You're welcome. I think I've tallied this correctly," she said, counting out what she owed him.

"You don't need to pay for it," he said, pushing the coins back toward her.

"Yes, Luther, I do need to pay for it. You'll need to replenish your stock, and that costs money. I promise to allow you the same privilege if you eat a meal in our restaurant," she said.

"No free meals, huh?" he asked, giving her a lopsided grin.

"I'm afraid not. At least not until we see if we can make a go of it," she replied.

"There's no doubt in my mind you'll make a go of it. There's plenty of hungry men in these parts, and once they've tasted your cooking, the word will spread like wildfire."

Maura felt a blush rise in her cheeks. It was the first time he had ever acknowledged that she was a good cook. Not that he hadn't eaten with a hearty appetite, for he'd surely done that. But it was the first verbal compliment she'd received from him. Although she wasn't sure exactly why, it pleased her immensely.

"I've got the coffee on. Would you care for a cup?" he asked, watching as she moved toward the peg where her cloak was hanging.

"Thanks, but I'd better be getting back. We plan to get started on our sewing this evening," Maura replied, fastening the woolen outer garment.

"Some other time then?" he questioned.

"Yes, some other time," she replied.

&.

"I think he realizes what a prize he lost," Georgette stated firmly as the two women sat sewing several hours later.

Maura and Georgette had been discussing the events that had occurred while Maura was at Luther's store earlier in the day.

"I doubt he'd ever think of me as a prize. He probably has just come to the realization that although I can't move as quickly as others, I did provide him a measure of assistance. At least he could leave the store for short periods of time when I was there," Maura said.

"What do you think?" Maura asked, holding one of the curtains in front of a dining room window.

"They're going to be ideal," Georgette replied. "I'm glad you chose this heavy lace fabric. I wasn't sure when I first saw it, but it's exactly what we need."

"I think the dark green tassels on the curtains, along with the dark green tablecloths, will set off the oak furniture to perfection," Maura remarked.

"Michael Blanchard asked me if I would attend a gathering at the minister's house Friday night," Georgette announced, unexpectedly changing the subject.

"How exciting. You told him you'd go, didn't you?"

"No. I told him I wasn't interested in any type of courtship."

"Georgette! Why did you say that? He's been so kind to us, and he's a nice man."

"I told you a few days ago that I'm not interested in men right now. I have Becca and you and our new business venture," she replied.

"You're also entitled to a little fun in your life. Just because he occasionally escorts you doesn't mean that you're obligated to enter into a courtship. So long as he knows all you're interested in is friendship, what's the harm?"

"I'm a mother, and I need to be with Becca. What will I say if he asks about my circumstances?"

"Tell him in a kind manner that you don't care to discuss your personal business, and I'm sure he'll honor your wishes. As to needing to be with Becca, you'd be gone only three or four hours. Becca won't even know you've left the house, and I hope you would trust me to care for her," Maura encouraged.

"I wouldn't feel right leaving you alone, especially during the holiday season. It seems improper for me to go out enjoying myself while you would be here caring for my baby."

"I want you to go and have some fun, Georgette. Tell Michael you'll go as long as he doesn't interpret your acceptance as anything more than friendship."

"Well. . .if you insist. It really does sound like fun," Georgette acquiesced.

"Good. Now, tell me what they've planned for the evening," Maura encouraged.

"We're going to have a taffy pull and make popcorn. Then later everyone will gather around the piano and sing carols. Michael said that he went last year and it was great fun."

"It sounds like a wonderful holiday celebration. I'm glad you've agreed to attend," Maura said.

"It appears we've reached a good stopping point for this evening, and I think I hear Becca's familiar cry," Georgette replied.

"You go ahead. I'll finish folding these, and then I'll be going to bed, also," Maura answered.

"You're such a wonderful person, Maura. I thank God every

day for sending you into my life," Georgette said as she leaned down to give Maura a hug.

"Thank you, Georgette. You and Becca have been a blessing to me also, and the three of us are going to be just fine. Hurry now and feed your baby before she thinks you've deserted her," Maura said, returning the hug.

During the following days, the women fell into a routine of caring for Becca, cleaning, sewing, and testing the recipes they would place on their menu, both the regular fare and the daily specials they wanted to offer. It proved to be great fun, although several of the dishes had ended up as dinner for the large tan dog who had recently adopted them and now made his home outside in their backyard. They had named him Waffles, partly because of his pale brown coloring, but mainly because the first meal he'd received had been a batch of burned waffles they'd thrown out the back door. He'd eaten every bite, and the women had been calling him Waffles ever since. He'd follow them whenever they didn't scold and send him back home. But the dog seemed particularly protective of Becca. His tail would wag continuously when Georgette carried the baby outdoors, and if Becca cried, the dog would yelp until she was quieted. If a stranger approached the back door or he thought anything unseemly was occurring near the house, he barked profusely until Maura or Georgette assured him everything was all right.

Maura and Georgette had discussed the possibility that Waffles might present some problems once they opened the restaurant, but for now his presence was welcome.

When Friday evening arrived, Maura eagerly assisted Georgette as she prepared for the party. The dress she had chosen was a cherry red tissue silk with a bertha of ivory lace-bordered gauze. The cuffs and skirt were embroidered in a deep green diamond design, and Georgette fashioned her hair into a chignon of pale blond curls fastened by a deep green ribbon and small red roses. She was a beautiful young lady, and the excitement of an evening out had added a touch of color to her cheeks.

"Are you sure you don't mind staying with Becca?" she asked for the third time that evening, just as Michael's knock sounded at the front door.

Hearing the sound, Waffles barked and came loping onto the front porch. "Stop that barking before you wake up the baby! You know Michael," Maura admonished the dog. "Come in, Michael. Sorry for Waffles's greeting, but at least he didn't jump on you and ruin your suit. Georgette will be down in just a moment," she told him.

Hearing her footsteps, Michael turned and watched as Georgette came down the staircase and into the foyer.

"You look—" but he stopped midsentence, seeing the look she gave him.

"—very friendly," he finished, not knowing what else to say.

All three of them burst into laughter. "Thank you, Michael. You look very friendly also," Georgette replied with a giggle.

Michael held her brown velvet-trimmed cloak as Georgette slipped her arms inside. Looking into the hallway mirror, she carefully tied the matching velvet bonnet, then placed a kiss on Becca's forehead. Georgette and Michael bid Maura good-bye and headed off toward the Wilsons'. Maura watched through the opalescent glass window until they were out of sight and then placed the sleeping baby in her cradle. Pulling her rocking chair closer to the fireplace, she began sewing the last set of curtains for the dining room.

# seven

Georgette and Michael made a most striking couple, although there was little competition. In fact, she and Mrs. Wilson were the sum total of the women at the gathering. Mrs. Wilson divulged that she'd invited Luther, hopeful that he'd bring Maura, but he had politely declined. In a town the size of Placerville there were few women, and the remainder who had been invited were unable to attend for one reason or another.

"I probably waited until too close to Christmas. Next year I'll have it earlier," she told Georgette, attempting to explain why the five other women weren't in attendance.

There was, however, no shortage of male guests. It seemed that the single men of the church were more than available to enjoy an evening of homespun holiday festivity.

"Your house looks lovely, and the tree is quite beautiful," Georgette complimented, although the branches were void of any ornamentation.

"Thank you, Georgette. I thought we'd make a few decorations this evening and decorate the tree if our guests wanted to help. Most of the men don't have an opportunity to participate in the familiar holiday activities they were accustomed to during childhood, so I thought they might find it fun," she confided.

"I don't know about the men, but it sounds like fun to me," Georgette replied.

"Charles, since you and the men are gathered at the fireplace anyway, why don't you begin making some popcorn? When it has cooled—and if you gentlemen haven't eaten all of it—we'll string some for the tree."

It was obvious that Edith Wilson was an organizer. Pulling

out strips of wrapping paper that she had painted, she set several of the men to work making chains. Next she produced a large bowl of cranberries to be strung and a large container of gingerbread men and stars that she had baked the day before. Another container held cornucopias she'd made out of an old box. They'd been decorated with ribbon, lace, and velvet scraps, ending up as pretty ornaments. Yet another box contained candle holders that her father had hammered out of tin and given to her for her first Christmas tree after she'd been married.

"I've used them every year. Now that Papa's dead, they mean even more to me," she explained to Georgette, who nodded, not because she'd shared the same experience, but because the girl wanted to avoid appearing obtuse.

*I wonder what she'd think of my father's last gift to me?* Georgette thought. *A one-way ticket out of his life. Much easier than dealing with the embarrassment of a daughter who was pregnant out of wedlock.*

"How did you happen to come to Placerville?" Edith inquired, as if she'd been reading Georgette's thoughts.

There was a silent pause, but just then Michael came up behind her. "I'm here for a lesson on how to get the string through these gingerbread men," he announced as he sat down beside her.

"How did you come to choose that particular task?" she asked with a grin.

"I figured I'd get to eat the ones I break," he admitted sheepishly.

"I believe there must be a small part of little boys that never quite turns into men," Mrs. Wilson said with a chuckle. "You instruct him, Georgette, while I see if there's going to be any popcorn left to string for the tree."

"Are you having a pleasant time?" Michael asked, carefully watching as Georgette used her needle to enlarge the hole Mrs. Wilson had made while baking the cookies. Carefully she threaded the string through the hole and tied it in a knot.

"Yes, I'm having a wonderful time. Now, let's see if you learned anything," she said, handing him a needle and sliding the pieces of string toward him.

"You can't push quite that hard," she said, when his first attempt resulted in a decapitated gingerbread man.

"While I'm eating this one, perhaps you should give me another lesson," he suggested, causing Georgette to laugh.

*It feels so good to laugh over such a simple thing as a broken cookie,* she thought, deftly using the needle to enlarge the holes in ten of the cookies while Michael sat watching.

"Aren't you going to leave any for me?" he finally asked as she continued working.

"I think your talents may run in other directions. Why don't you see if you can pull the string through the top without breaking any more," she amicably requested.

"I think this is merely a plot to keep me from eating the cookies," he whispered loudly enough for the group to hear. Although they laughed along with him, none of them offered him any compassion. They were busy stringing popcorn and attaching the candle holders with only each other for company. It was difficult to sympathize with the only unmarried man in the room who was escorting a beautiful woman.

When they had finished decorating the tree, the group moved into the kitchen to begin pulling the taffy that Edith had made and placed on the table to cool just a bit.

"Georgette, put this apron over your dress. I don't want this taffy pull to be the cause of staining that beautiful gown," Mrs. Wilson said, holding out a sateen apron with ribbon embroidery.

"This apron is as pretty as my dress, Edith. I don't think I want to chance staining it, either. Don't you have an old one I won't worry about?"

"Of course she does," Charles asserted, pulling a faded cambric apron from a hook near the back door.

"Charles," she called, attempting to sound outraged at his actions.

"Oh, we don't need to put on airs. Georgette will be just as happy in this old apron as your fancy holiday finery," he said, giving his wife a kiss on the cheek.

"He's right, Edith. Now, I feel like I'm ready to get to work on that taffy."

Georgette wasn't sure why, but by the time they had finished the candy, a nagging uneasiness was beginning to plague her.

"I think I should leave now that we've finished the candy," she told Edith as she removed the apron and hung it back on the hook.

"Oh, please don't leave so early. We're going to light the candles on the tree and sing carols. The decorations look so pretty, and once we light the candles, there's a whole different atmosphere. I'm sure Maura is delighted to have some time with the baby; in fact, I know she'd want you to stay for the very best part of the evening. Besides, I've made a chestnut pudding that you haven't even tasted," Edith cajoled.

Georgette glanced at Michael with a questioning look in her eyes.

"It's up to you," he told her. "I'd like to have you stay and enjoy yourself, but if you're feeling anxious, we'll leave whenever you're ready."

She had hoped he would make the decision for her. Obviously he was wise for his years and realized that if he said they should stay while something was amiss at home, she'd hold it against him. On the other hand, if he said they should leave and everything was fine at home, it would be his fault that she missed the most meaningful portion of the evening.

"I guess I'm just being silly since this is my first time away from Becca for more than an hour," she told Edith and Michael.

"So you'll stay?" Edith asked, clapping her hands.

"Yes, I'll stay," Georgette answered, a warmth enveloping

her when she realized how much she was actually wanted.

Before she could change her mind, Edith decided they should have dessert and then sing carols before returning home. She carried a beautiful silver tray bearing her glazed chestnut pudding into the dining room and was greeted by the expected ohs and ahs of all in attendance. The pudding had been baked in a fluted mold and inverted on the platter and was now covered with a delectable-looking punch sauce and surrounded by waxed holly leaves and berries.

"My sister sent me the chestnuts from back East. I wrote her last spring telling her I longed to have our mother's famous chestnut pudding for Christmas, and low and behold, a box arrived just last week. I had nearly given up on receiving them," she told the group as she dished the pudding onto china dessert dishes.

"It tastes even better than it looks," one of the men remarked after they'd all been served and Pastor Wilson had said a short prayer.

"I don't believe I've ever heard of chestnut pudding, Edith, but it is luscious. Perhaps you'd be willing to share your recipe with me, and if we're fortunate enough to find a supply of chestnuts, we could serve it at the restaurant."

Edith beamed at the idea and, before anyone could stop her, began enumerating the elaborate details of how to make the pudding. "First you boil the chestnuts just long enough to peel them easily," she began. "Once you've gotten them peeled, you want to cook them in milk—not a lot of milk—just barely enough to cover the chestnuts, and you must be sure to add half a cinnamon stick to the milk. . ."

"Perhaps it would be easier for Georgette to remember the recipe if you'd write it down for her tomorrow," her husband interrupted, realizing that the men weren't the least bit interested in how to make a chestnut pudding. "Why don't we move over to the piano, and I'll light the candles while the rest of you begin singing?" he tactfully suggested.

"How silly of me, prattling on like that," Edith replied. "I'll write it out for you," she told Georgette as the two of them walked toward the piano. Seating herself, she began playing "O Little Town of Bethlehem," and soon all of them were singing while Charles carefully lit the candles. "Silent Night" was followed by "We Three Kings" and "Joy to the World."

"I really must be leaving. The tree is so pretty and it's been such a joyous evening, but it's getting late," Georgette whispered to Michael as they finished the last stanza of "Joy to the World."

Without saying a word, he moved from her side and gathered her cloak and bonnet and brought them to her, while the others continued singing.

"Must you leave us?" Charles asked while Georgette was tying her bonnet.

"I truly must get home, but it's been one of the most wonderful nights of my life," she told them. Impulsively, she walked to where Edith sat on the piano stool and gave her a hug. "Thank you, Edith, for making me so welcome in your home."

"It was my pleasure," she answered. "We'll sing you out the door," she told them and struck up the chords to "God Rest Ye Merry Gentlemen" just as a pounding sounded at the door.

❧

Luther worked late Friday night, just as he had most nights since Maura had moved out. There were a few town folks that were doing a bit of Christmas shopping or buying necessities to make their gifts while others would come in later in the day when their other chores were completed. Some of the miners who were in town for supplies or just to get drunk came to the store whether it was day or evening. If they saw so much as a lantern burning, they figured the store was open.

After Luther and Maura had married, she had been responsible for completing the paperwork and performing the accounting for the mercantile each evening after dinner. However, when she moved out, Luther was once again required to assume these thankless tasks. Instead of doing the paperwork after returning home, he preferred to work on it at the store as he had time between customers and stocking the shelves. Sometimes, on nights like tonight, when most of the decent town folk were at home preparing for Christmas or over at the Wilsons' enjoying a holiday gathering, he'd work late and finish up before returning home for the night.

*I probably should have asked Maura,* he thought to himself as he tallied a column of figures, but knew he didn't want to take the chance of being rejected. He'd attended the Wilsons' annual gathering every year since he'd arrived in Placerville, but it was different this year. He was afraid someone might question him about his marriage if he were in a more relaxed setting. Luther was all business while in his store, and people immediately sensed that about him. They never attempted to probe into his personal life while he was working, and he liked it that way. In fact, he didn't want people delving into his personal affairs at any time, but he knew in a small town that was impossible.

It was ten-thirty when he finally decided to close the store and make the brief walk home. However, he had walked only a short distance when he heard the eerie howling of a dog in the distance. It stopped and then began again. As he continued down the crooked street, he glanced toward the house that Maura and Georgette had purchased. It had become a habit. He despised himself for it, but hard as he tried, he couldn't keep from looking toward their new home each time he left the store.

There appeared to be an oil lamp burning, but that wasn't unusual. *Maura's probably still sewing on her tablecloths and curtains,* he thought. He had learned that she was an ambitious woman, rising early and staying up at night until all of her chores were done. *Probably learned that at an early age, what with it taking her longer to do things,* he reflected.

A sudden movement on the front porch caught his eye as he

turned toward the house one last time. Straining his eyes, he attempted to make out the figure stirring about on the front porch. And then it came to him. The howling was Waffles, the stray dog that had attached himself to the women shortly after they'd moved into the house, and he was pacing back and forth on the front porch.

Luther quickened his pace and then broke into a run toward the house. As he drew closer he could see that the glass in the front door had been smashed and the door was now standing ajar. However, there was no sign of Maura or Georgette. As he began to run up the steps, Waffles bared his teeth and emitted a low guttural snarl.

*Great!* Luther thought. *How am I supposed to get past this dog and see if anything's wrong?* After several attempts at coaxing the dog into allowing him past, he became completely exasperated.

"Waffles, sit!" he yelled at the dog in his sternest voice.

Immediately the dog retreated into a sitting position and allowed him to enter the house. Becca was crying, and as soon as Luther entered the house, Waffles ran ahead of him to the bedroom, apparently sensing that Luther would help. It was obvious the dog wanted him to hurry. Spotting Becca in her cradle, Luther quickly judged that she appeared to be in no apparent danger. Except for the cold air that had been drifting in through the front door, nothing seemed out of order. Luther grabbed a quilt from Georgette's bed and placed it around the baby. That would have to do until he could find Maura.

"Where is she?" he asked the dog, frustrated since he'd not found her with Becca.

Luther was startled when the dog took off running up the stairs toward one of the bedrooms. Following Waffles's lead, he raced up the steps but momentarily stopped in the doorway, overcome by the sight. The room had been completely ransacked, and Maura was lying on the floor, with a small pool of blood by her head.

Stooping down, he carefully lifted her onto the bed and felt for a pulse. Her breathing seemed shallow, but she was alive. *Where is Georgette?* he wondered, knowing that the women were seldom far apart.

"Is Georgette here?" he asked the dog, feeling like a fool.

The dog didn't move from Maura's side, which Luther took as a sign no one else was in the house. And then he remembered the Wilsons' party. Michael Blanchard had mentioned that he would like to ask Georgette to the party. Afraid to leave and yet not sure when Georgette would return, Luther didn't know what to do.

"I guess you're it," he said to the dog. "Stay!" he commanded, pointing at the animal, hoping it would remain with Maura long enough for him to find Georgette. Relieved when the dog didn't rise to follow him, he hurried downstairs. Scooping up the baby, he wrapped the heavy quilt around her for protection and headed toward the Wilsons' parsonage.

He could hear the strains of "God Rest Ye Merry Gentlemen" as he approached the house and banged on the front door.

# eight

"Luther! What's happened? What's wrong with the baby?" Georgette cried out in a voice filled with panic. "Where's Maura?" she screamed, looking past him but not seeing her friend.

"Give him a chance to answer," Michael consoled quietly.

"There's no time—Maura needs a doctor, and I've got to return to the house. I left her there alone. One of you men go for Doc Simmons—and tell him to hurry!" he commanded, shoving Becca into Georgette's open arms.

"The baby appears to be fine, but you might want to remain here with Mrs. Wilson for a while," he stated as an afterthought and then took off running toward the house.

"I think I should go back to the house," Georgette told Michael and Mrs. Wilson, looking at both of them for confirmation.

"It's safer for you and the baby to remain here, my dear," Mrs. Wilson replied, "at least until we find out what's going on."

"That's just it! I can't stand not knowing how Maura is and if there's some way I could be helping her," Georgette replied as Becca began to cry.

"Michael, why don't you go to the house and check on the situation? By the time Georgette has finished feeding the baby, you should be back with a report for us," Mrs. Wilson suggested.

"Oh, that's a wonderful idea, Edith!" Georgette exclaimed. "Would you do that for me, Michael?" she asked.

"Of course, he will," Edith answered for him, while guiding him toward the door. "If the news is bad, don't tell her all the details immediately. We'll need to soften the blow a bit so that she doesn't become overly anxious," Mrs. Wilson whispered to Michael as they reached the front porch.

He nodded his head in understanding and pulled his coat tightly around him as he hurried away.

"The baby is soaking wet," Georgette remarked as she removed the heavy quilt that Luther had wrapped around Becca.

"Don't worry, dear. I have some soft white tea towels. You can use one of those. Becca will never know the difference," Edith answered, going to the kitchen and quickly returning with the substitute diaper.

"Thank you, Edith," Georgette murmured, though her thoughts remained on Maura's condition.

"Oh, look—her wrapper is soaked, too. Let me see what I can find," Edith offered, although not sure that Georgette was even listening to her.

A short time later Edith reappeared, carrying two pieces of soft flannel and a blanket.

"I'm afraid I don't have much in the way of baby clothes, but why don't you wrap her tightly in these pieces of flannel? Then we can use the larger blanket to keep her snug."

Georgette smiled. Edith was fluttering about like a mother hen taking care of a brood of chicks.

"Did I say something amusing?" Edith asked, seeing Georgette's smile.

"No, I was just watching you scurry about helping me. I'm so appreciative of your kindness, Edith. Do you think it's a good sign that Michael hasn't returned yet?"

"He hasn't been gone more than twenty minutes, dear. You must remember that until Maura is able to talk, there won't be much to tell. It may take the doctor a while before he can give us any kind of prognosis. I know you feel very helpless right now, and so do I. But the two of us can do the most important thing of all. We can pray," Edith reminded her young friend.

And pray they did! From the moment Edith made the pronouncement until they heard a stirring at the front door.

Charles Wilson led Michael and two of the other men into the parlor, all of them sober-faced.

"Tell me!" Georgette cried, rising from her chair. "Tell me that she's all right, please."

"She's alive, but she hasn't regained consciousness just yet," Michael softly answered, moving to Georgette's side. "The doctor said there was only superficial bleeding, but he couldn't be sure that there wasn't some internal bleeding or trauma to the brain itself. It appeared that she was struck with some type of blunt instrument, and we don't know how long she was lying there unconscious."

"Michael! I told you not to go into all the unpleasant details. It will only cause Georgette to become overly anxious," Edith chastised the young man.

Michael's face turned crimson at her reproach; then he looked toward Georgette to see if she had gone into shock or fainted from his remarks.

"She's not a wilting flower, Edith," her husband said. "If anyone has a need—in fact a right—to know what is going on, it's Georgette. I think she'd be more upset at Michael for withholding information from her, wouldn't you, child?" the pastor inquired, seeking the girl's affirmation.

Georgette was beginning to feel as though she were being dissected by the pastor and his wife, yet she knew they were both just trying to protect her. Having to side with either of them would be uncomfortable.

"Edith, I think it's probably best that I know the full extent of Maura's injuries and what awaits me when I return home. Hearing the news, although upsetting, is easier to bear while I am here surrounded by such loving friends," she diplomatically responded.

"Well, of course, dear. I was just afraid that if you became too upset, Becca would sense it and become fretful. But I see you are of a stronger character than I thought."

Georgette smiled benevolently and turned to Michael. "She's going to need me there to care for her. How soon will the doctor be leaving?"

"To be honest, the doctor has already left. He started home at the same time we did," Michael answered.

"What? Get my cloak, Michael, and I'll get Becca. How could you leave her alone like that?" she rebuked the group of men standing in the parlor.

"Georgette, you need to calm yourself. Surely you know we wouldn't have left Maura alone. Luther is with her. The doctor gave him a list of instructions, and he insisted that he would remain to care for her. When we left, he had pulled the rocking chair close by her bed, and Waffles was curled by his feet."

"Luther? You left Maura to Luther's care? What were you thinking—or were any of you thinking?"

"He's her husband, Georgette. He's the one who should be with her," Michael reminded her in a conciliatory tone.

"He may be her husband, but as far as I'm concerned, he doesn't act like one. Besides, come morning his primary concern will be the Buchanan Mercantile—not his wife! Michael, you can escort me or not, as you choose, but I am going home right now!" she defiantly responded.

It was obvious that she wasn't going to be dissuaded, at least not by anyone at the pastor's house.

"I'll get your cloak," Michael immediately replied and then hastened to fetch it.

"And I'll get the baby," Edith offered. "I'd be happy to come along and remain at the house with you—in fact, we both would, wouldn't we, Charles?"

"Wouldn't we what?" he asked, having grown accustomed to only half-listening when his wife spoke.

"Charles! We wouldn't mind staying over with Georgette and Maura tonight, would we?" she asked, giving him a look that implied that she expected only one answer.

"Well, no, we wouldn't mind, but Luther is there, and I don't think they need a complete houseful of people upsetting their routine," he answered.

"What do you think, Georgette? Would you like us to stay with you?" Edith suggested.

"Thank you for the offer, but Charles is right. Luther is already at the house and—"

"But what if the baby is awake during the night so that you can't get any rest? Come morning, if Luther leaves to tend the store, you'll be tired and with no help to care for Becca and Maura," she rebutted.

"Why don't you go along, Edith?" Charles suggested. "I won't mind, but I don't think there's any need for me to intrude."

It was obvious that Edith was going to insist until Georgette relented. In order to put a halt to the bantering, Georgette acquiesced.

"Michael is going to escort me home now, Edith. I'll be looking for you after you've had a chance to put together a few things for the night," Georgette said.

"Charles will escort me over—it won't take me but a few minutes," she replied, already scurrying out of the room to begin her preparations.

"She means well," Charles said to Georgette as they reached the front door.

"Of course she does, and I'm sure I'll be glad that she insisted on keeping me company," Georgette remarked.

"Thank you for all your help, and thank you for the wonderful evening. I'm sorry it had to be marred by this tragedy. Strange, but it seems a lifetime ago that we were singing carols, doesn't it?" she asked and then bid Charles good night.

As they neared the house, Georgette's steps began to slow. "What's that over the door?" she asked.

"The window was broken out in the front door. Luther put boards over it until the glass can be replaced," Michael replied.

"You mean whoever broke into the house also broke out the window?" Georgette asked, a chill climbing her spine.

"Luther doesn't think so. He thinks that Waffles broke it out."

"Waffles? Where did he get an idea like that?"

"Seems the dog had a pretty good-sized lump on his head and some cuts around his face and front paws," he answered. "Course, nobody's sure of anything right now."

She nodded her head as they walked up the front steps and cautiously entered the house.

"Who's there?" Luther called, coming to the top of the steps.

"It's me, Luther, Georgette—and Michael is with me," she answered. "I'm going to put Becca in bed. Would it be all right if I come up to see Maura?"

He nodded his head. "You leaving?" Luther questioned Michael in a manner indicating his departure was expected.

"In just a few minutes. I plan to wait and bid Georgette good night," he replied, surprised at Luther's tone. "You'd think this was his house," he murmured when Luther returned to Maura's room.

"What did you say?" Georgette asked.

"I was just telling Luther I'd be leaving as soon as I bid you good night."

"Oh. I thought I heard you say something about the house," she replied.

"I know you want to get upstairs and see Maura, so I won't keep you any longer. I do want you to know how much I enjoyed spending the evening with you at the Wilsons'. I'm just sorry all this unhappiness had to occur. I hope you'll allow me to stop by and see how all of you are doing and permit me to do anything I can to help," he offered, his voice hopeful.

"Of course, please stop by. I can't promise perfect hospitality, but I'm sure that under the circumstances, you'll understand," she answered. "Thank you for this evening, Michael.

I'm sorry to rush you off, but I do want to get upstairs and see Maura."

"I understand," he said. "Be sure to bolt the door after Edith arrives," he instructed protectively.

She nodded and then turned and ran up the steps.

Quietly she tiptoed into the room. Waffles came toward her, wagging his tail and looking a bit the worse for his experience. She leaned down and started to pat him but then stopped short, not wanting to hurt him.

"Good dog, Waffles," she said as he licked her hand.

"Maura?" she whispered. "Maura, it's me, Georgette. Can you hear me?"

"She's still unconscious," Luther answered. "She moved a little just before you got here, but that's been the extent of it. The doctor said not to be overly concerned unless this continues for another day or so. I'm trying to believe him."

Georgette noticed that Luther was gently running his thumb back and forth over Maura's left hand. *Strange,* she thought. *He could barely stand to look at her withered arm before, but now that she's in a state of trauma, he's sitting here stroking it as though he loved her—flawed limbs included.*

"Mrs. Wilson insisted on spending the night. I tried to discourage her, but she wouldn't hear of it. Under the circumstances, it will prevent any idle gossip that might arise. She should be here soon, and I can sit with Maura while you get some rest. When Becca needs to be fed, you can come back and sit with Maura, and then I'll get some rest. If she should wake up, I'll come and get you immediately," Georgette stated.

"I guess that would work. I know you want to be with her, and I'm sure you'll be more comfortable if I'm not around. I'm sure you don't hold me in very high esteem."

"This isn't the time for us to discuss what I think of you, Luther. Right now, all I care about is that Maura gets the best care possible. I can put aside my feelings to ensure that," she replied, just as a rapping sounded at the front door.

Startled by the sound, Waffles began to bark and skittishly run in and out of the bedroom door.

"Hush, Waffles," Maura weakly commanded the dog.

Luther and Georgette turned simultaneously and looked at Maura. However, she didn't appear to have moved, and her eyes were still closed.

"Maura!" Luther called.

"Maura—can you hear me? Oh please, Maura, answer me," Georgette begged.

But she didn't move; in fact, not so much as an eyelash fluttered. They looked at each other, questioning whether they'd really heard anything; then the rapping at the front door sounded once again. This time, however, Waffles remained calm while Georgette went downstairs to answer the door.

"Sorry it took me so long, dear," Edith began apologizing the minute she bustled into the room. "Just point out where I should put these things and tell me what you want done. You can leave, Charles," she said, dismissing her husband and turning her full attention to Georgette.

Ignoring her, Charles moved toward Georgette. "Has there been any change?" he asked.

"Not really. Luther and I both thought we heard her speak a few minutes ago when you knocked on the door, but I'm beginning to think our imaginations got the best of us," she replied.

"I'll be praying. I'm sure that God is going to see both of you through this just fine. I'll be on my way, now," he said, leaning down to give his wife a peck on the cheek. "Good night, dear, I'll check on you in the morning."

"Good night," she answered and walked him to the door.

"Would you lock the bolt on the door, please?" Georgette requested as Edith closed the door. "I'm going to sit up with Maura until the baby wakens for her feeding. Why don't you sleep in my room since I may have difficulty hearing her when she wakens?"

"I'll come to get you when she's hungry," Edith replied, hastening to the bedroom on her appointed mission.

❧

It seemed only minutes had passed when Georgette's voice calling from the doorway awakened him from a restless sleep.

"I'm going downstairs to feed Becca and rest for a while. Do you want Edith to sit with Maura? She's still sleeping," Georgette informed Luther as he began to rise from the large overstuffed chair where he had been sleeping.

"No, I want to sit with her. You go ahead," he instructed while rubbing his eyes and moving toward Maura's bedroom.

He stood a moment staring down at his wife's lifeless form. He had treated her shabbily, and he knew it. *I've become as cruel and heartless as my father,* he thought as he walked to the side of the bed. The small oil lamp on the bedside table cast a flickering glow upon the pages of Maura's open Bible. Hoping to find comfort in the passages, he sat down and began to read.

"'God is our refuge and strength, an ever-present help in trouble,'" he quietly read aloud. "I'd guess you've been asking God for strength all your life—strength to deal with people just like me. People who judge you before ever giving you half a chance," he said to her sleeping figure.

"Now me, I've spent the last five years dwelling on my past, constantly attempting to prove my father wrong. It appears, however, that in my zeal to prove him incorrect, I've become just like him—an unrelenting taskmaster, void of love or compassion," he murmured.

*Dear God, forgive me,* he silently prayed as he continued his vigil.

## nine

After two long days and nights, Luther agreed to reopen the store. Pastor Wilson and several others had offered to volunteer their time to keep the mercantile open, but Luther knew it would be utter chaos. None of them knew his stock or prices; moreover, his inventory lists would be botched in no time, to say nothing of what would happen to the bookkeeping system without proper accounting at day's end.

Georgette sighed a breath of relief as he walked out the door. "I know he's trying to help and it's his place to be with Maura, but I'm glad to have him out from underfoot for a while," Georgette confided to Edith as the two of them began to clear away the kitchen dishes.

"I know, dear, but we must remember how distressed he must be to have his wife in such a condition. I can't even begin to think how I would feel if that were Charles," Edith responded.

"Edith! There is absolutely no parallel between your marriage to Charles and Maura's marriage to Luther. Quite frankly—and I know I shouldn't say this—I wonder why he's even here. He didn't want to be around her when she was healthy. Oh, I'm sorry, Edith," she apologized, seeing the look on the other woman's face.

"You don't need to apologize, Georgette. I know that you are deeply concerned about Maura; besides, you're worn out from lack of proper rest. But let me share with you one thing I've learned in my life—we humans give up on things a lot faster than the Lord does. He is so much more creative than we could ever imagine, and believe me—His plan will be revealed in His time.

"Luther and Maura are both Christians, and I believe that God will restore their marriage. It may not occur in an uncomplicated manner or in the near future, but when it happens, it will transpire because both of them have looked to Him for their answer. Now, I guess I'd better get upstairs," she said, abruptly ending her discourse and wiping her hands on a dish towel.

"Thank you, Edith. I've not been very charitable to Luther. In fact, I've been downright rude at times. You've convinced me that I need to be praying for Luther rather than judging his behavior," she remarked, with thoughts of her past rushing through her mind.

"We'll both pray for him! He won't be able to resist if we're both soliciting God's help," she said, chuckling heartily.

It was midafternoon, and Edith had gone home for several hours. Having carried the cradle upstairs, Georgette sat stitching on the last of the tablecloths as Becca slept. Waffles was curled up on the rug by Georgette's feet, keeping vigil, when a loud rapping sounded at the front door.

Startled by the noise, Georgette jumped from the chair, her sewing basket and contents falling to the floor and frightening the dog. Instantly Waffles started barking and wakened Becca, whose lusty cries almost drowned out the dog. The knocking sounded again, sending Waffles into another round of barks that was followed by Becca's wailing.

"What in the world is going on?" Maura asked, a look of surprise on her face. "Why is Waffles in the house, and why is everyone in my bedroom?"

"Maura! Oh, Maura, are you all right?" Georgette questioned, attempting to be heard over the barking dog and sobbing child.

Again the rapping began.

"Georgette, please go answer the door so that Becca and the dog will settle down," Maura commanded. "Here, I'll hold Becca," she said, reaching to take the baby.

Noting Georgette's hesitation, she looked confused.

"What is wrong with you, Georgette?"

"Let me answer the door, and then I'll be right back to explain," the perplexed girl answered without turning over the baby.

Georgette rushed down the steps; Waffles came running behind her and skidded to a halt in front of the door, the ever-ready protector.

"It's just Edith and Charles. Now stop your barking," Georgette chastised the animal.

"I was beginning to get worried," Edith said, immediately lifting Becca from her mother's arms and crooning to the child. "Did our knocking waken her?"

"It was that or my dropping the sewing basket or Waffles barking at the top of his lungs," Georgette said, giving them a small laugh. "You're never going to believe this, but all the commotion seems to have awakened Maura. I need to get back upstairs right away."

"Here, Charles, you take the baby, and I'll go up with Georgette and see what's happening," she instructed, passing the baby to him in spite of the fact that he had no experience with infants.

Watching the two women walk up the steps and not sure what else to do, he stepped into the parlor, seated himself in the rocking chair, and began singing quietly to the baby.

"Charles!" Edith called out as she returned to the parlor several minutes later. "You're just not going to believe this, but Maura is back with us and seems fit as a fiddle. Here—give me the baby and go fetch Luther," she directed him but then stopped for a moment. "I'm sorry, dear. I'm so excited that I've forgotten my manners. Would you please go to the store and give Luther the news?"

"Of course, I will," he said giving her a peck on the cheek. "No need to apologize. I learned to live with your enthusiasm years ago."

"Enthusiasm. Now that's a nice word for it, isn't it?" she pondered aloud as Charles walked out the door.

❧

Charles made the short walk to the mercantile in record time, noting that there didn't seem to be any customers in the store as he entered the front door.

"I've good news," he called out, spotting Luther squatted down stocking shelves at the far end of the room.

"What? What's happened?"

"Maura has regained consciousness, and Edith sent me to fetch you. I'd be happy to watch after things here at the store, if you'd like," the pastor suggested. "Or I guess you could put a sign on the door for a while," he suggested, observing Luther's hesitance.

"What? Oh, no, I've no problem with you tending the store, Charles—in fact, I appreciate your kind offer. It's just so—" he said, unable to complete the sentence.

"Miraculous?" the pastor suggested.

"Yes—that, too," Luther agreed, not sure that miraculous was quite the word he had been searching for. "If you're certain that it's not an imposition, I would like to see her. I won't stay long."

"Stay as long as you like. I think I'll be more adept at running your store than performing several of the other chores Edith has thrust upon me lately," he remarked.

Georgette was just completing the amazing tale of how Waffles had been howling on the front porch the night of Maura's mishap when Luther strode into the room.

"Didn't figure there was any need to knock on the door and cause one of you to run downstairs," Luther explained as the three women looked toward him, silent. "Charles came over and told me the news," he continued.

"Perhaps we should give you two an opportunity to talk alone. Why don't you sit here," Edith suggested, rising from the chair beside the bed and moving toward the door.

"Thank you, Edith," Luther responded, seating himself.

"Isn't it about time to feed Becca?" Edith asked, looking at Georgette.

"No. Ohhh, she may be hungry," Georgette replied, seeing the look on Edith's face.

"I'm sorry, Edith. Sometimes I'm so dimwitted," Georgette whispered as the two women walked down the steps.

"You are not dimwitted or anything even closely related to it! I realized you didn't hear me, so I just gave you a little nudge. I believe that must be some more of my enthusiasm Charles was talking about earlier," she said, patting Georgette's hand and chuckling heartily.

❧

"It was kind of you to come so quickly," Maura said, though not sure why Luther had hurried to her bedside.

"I've been very concerned about you, Maura. In fact, I didn't return to the store until this morning when Georgette and Edith insisted. I don't know what Georgette told you before I came in, but you gave all of us a real fright. Do you recall any of what happened the other night?"

"I think so, although I almost wish I didn't," she answered, reaching up to touch her head.

"Will you tell me?" he asked, reaching to take her hand.

Startled, she pulled away.

"Maura, did he—did he hurt you?"

"Not in the way you're thinking," she replied, realizing that he had incorrectly interpreted her reaction to his touch. "Georgette tells me that you're the one responsible for finding me and getting help. Thank you for what you did."

"I'm just thankful that Waffles was making such a racket and caught my attention out there on the front porch. Do you feel up to talking about it?" he cajoled in a tender voice.

*Perhaps that knock on the head did cause a memory lapse,* Maura thought, confused by Luther's sudden change of behavior.

"I'll just sit here quietly," he remarked when she didn't immediately respond.

"I feel well enough to talk about it, Luther, and I don't think my memory is impaired—although you're not acting like the man I remember, so perhaps it is," she replied.

Without further hesitation, she began to recall the events that had occurred several nights earlier.

"Michael had escorted Georgette to the party at the Wilsons' and Becca was asleep in her cradle. I wanted to finish hemming the tablecloths and decided to stay up until they were completed. Besides, I didn't want to leave Becca downstairs, but I couldn't carry her cradle up—well, that doesn't matter. Anyway, I heard someone outside on the porch; then there was a tapping at the front door. Before I could get to the door, a man burst in and—"

"You mean you didn't have the door bolted?" he interrupted.

"No, I didn't have the door bolted," she replied defensively. "I didn't know when Georgette would be coming home, and I didn't want her to stand outside waiting for me to answer the door if I was in the bedroom with Becca. Besides, we never bolt the door until retiring for the night. Neither of us has had any cause to be frightened," she continued.

"Maura! With all the men coming through town, do you think that two women alone are safe?"

"Do you want to hear what happened or lecture me on my susceptibility to strangers in Placerville?"

"I'm sorry. Go on with your recollections," he apologized, giving her a reticent look.

"As I was saying, a man burst in the front door and told me to be quiet. As soon as he got inside, he slammed the door behind him. When I asked what he wanted, he said he was down on his luck, telling me he'd been searching for gold without any success. I offered him work roofing the house, but he just laughed and asked me why he should work when he could just take my money. When I told him I didn't have any money, he became angry and threatened me.

"Becca awakened and I was afraid he would hurt her, so I told him I might be able to find a little money upstairs. He followed me, and I took what money I had in my reticule and offered it to him. Angry because it was such a small amount, he began cursing and yelling, his voice growing louder and louder. Then he began pulling out drawers and slamming the furniture about, all the while shouting he was going to kill me if I didn't show him where my money was hidden. I screamed back at him, and the next thing I heard was glass breaking. Suddenly Waffles came running into the room and attacked the man—"

"Did he actually bite the intruder?" Luther asked.

"I'm not sure, although he had his teeth bared and was growling when he lunged at the man. I don't recall anything after that," she replied, sinking back onto her pillow.

"I've tired you out too much. It was too soon for you to go through the ordeal of recounting the events," he said apologetically.

"No, it's probably better this way. I might have forgotten or distorted some of the events if I hadn't told someone immediately, although I am feeling somewhat weak. Perhaps Edith could bring me a little something to eat. I think that might help."

"Of course. How thoughtless of me. You haven't eaten in close to three days now. It's no wonder you're weak. I'll go down and see what they can rustle up for you," he said, rising from the chair.

"Thank you," she replied. "And, Luther—you need not feel obligated to visit. I'll be fine. Georgette and Edith won't allow me to starve to death, and you have your business to look after," she added.

"Does that mean I'm unwelcome?" he asked, appearing to be pained by her words.

"It doesn't mean you're unwelcome. It means merely that I

know you have come out of your feeling of Christian duty and responsibility because I am your wife—at least by the letter of the law—"

"And in the eyes of God," he interrupted.

"Definitely in the eyes of God, Luther. Just not in your eyes or your heart," she said, turning her gaze from him.

"How can you become a wife in my eyes and heart if you won't even allow me to visit?" he asked in a defensive tone.

"Whenever you want to visit me out of more than pity or a sense of duty, you are welcome. Until then, it's best you stay away," she answered.

"I didn't want to intrude, but I thought you might be hungry. Oh, Luther! I almost ran into you," Edith said as she approached the doorway where Luther was standing.

"I was just coming down to tell you that Maura was hungry," Luther told the older woman.

"Don't let me rush you off. I'll just set up this tray and be out of here," Edith said as Luther moved around her.

"I was leaving anyway. Take care of yourself, Maura. If there's anything you need, send word," he instructed, the thumping of his footsteps and slamming of the front door providing final evidence of his departure.

❧

Maura quickly regained her strength; and although the women agreed that the restaurant would not open until after Christmas, they couldn't forego the opportunity to entertain with a dinner party on Christmas Day. The Wilsons, Ballards, and Bergmans, as well as Michael and Luther, were all invited. Stanley Ballard operated the livery stable, Samuel Bergman was the new president of the Placerville Bank, and all of them regularly listened to Pastor Wilson on Sunday mornings. Georgette personally invited each of the couples and Michael.

"I didn't stop by the store. I thought you'd want to invite Luther personally," Georgette said upon returning to the house.

Maura watched as Georgette untied her dark blue bonnet and matching cape.

"Was I wrong?" Georgette asked when Maura didn't reply.

"He'll probably turn me down, and I'm not sure I can handle the humiliation."

"Maura Thorenson! I don't want to seem unkind, but I wonder how he felt when you told him he didn't need to bother visiting you. Seems I remember some passages from the Bible that we studied before I became a Christian. You're the one who taught me about forgiveness and God's grace. Do you remember what you said when I asked you how you could ever associate with the likes of me?"

"Of course, I do. I told you that it was always a privilege to be associated with another child of the kingdom. But those circumstances were completely different. You had just accepted Jesus as your Savior and were feeling so unworthy. On the other hand, Luther has been a Christian for years, but look at how he's treated me," Maura retorted defensively.

"Seems I recall something else you told me. Didn't you say that sometimes Christians are so unforgiving and critical of each other that Satan can just sit around and enjoy the chaos they create for themselves?"

"Georgette, I think you're manipulating some of my teaching, trying to make it fit a totally different situation!"

"Then why are you getting so upset? You know, Maura, you've been a Christian for years, too. It would appear to this newborn Christian that you both need to take a look at yourselves. I love you, Maura, but you're just as wrong as Luther. He's hurt you, and now you're not going to be happy until you've made him suffer for that," Georgette quietly answered.

"You've become quite an authority, haven't you? Let me tell you something, Georgette. You don't know what it's like to be different. You stand in front of me with a beautiful, whole body that any man would love. You haven't lived through years of being stared at and whispered about—children pointing you out to their parents as if you were some type of monstrosity. You've received looks of adoration while I've received stares of disdain. It's so easy for you to tell me I shouldn't worry about receiving further humiliation from my husband," Maura retorted, her voice having risen a full octave during the recitation.

"I'm sorry, Maura. What was I thinking of? Here I am upsetting you, when the last thing you need is to become distressed. I'll go and ask Luther, and if he says anything that makes me think he's coming out of pity, I'll retract the invitation," Georgette said, quickly removing her cape from the peg and placing it around her shoulders. "I'll be back in just a few minutes. You look after Becca for just a little longer," she instructed, tying the ribbons of her bonnet and then rushing out the front door before Maura could say anything further.

The cool air felt good against her cheeks as Georgette walked quickly toward the general store. *Why did I say those things to Maura? She's the only true friend I've ever had, and now she'll probably never speak to me again,* Georgette thought, the idea causing her to grimace.

"You look like you just lost your best friend," Luther called out when she walked in the store, the dour look still etched on her face.

"Perhaps I have," she murmured, not loud enough for him to hear.

"What'd you say? Couldn't quite make out what you said," he replied, moving from the far end of the store toward her.

"Oh, nothing. I was just deep in thought. Maura and I were wondering if you would like to join us for Christmas dinner. The Wilsons, Ballards, and Bergmans have all agreed to attend, and, of course, Michael will be there," she quickly explained.

"Sounds like you've gathered most of the businessmen and their wives," he answered with a smile.

"Not quite. The majority of the businesses in Placerville will be open on Christmas. I don't think the saloons and gambling halls ever close their doors, do you?"

"Not if there's any chance of making money, they don't. And I imagine you're right. A lot of the miners will be feeling melancholy and will come to town hoping to drown their holiday loneliness in liquor," he replied.

"That's such a shame," Georgette answered, as an idea began to form. "You know, Luther, it would be wonderful if there were an alternative—something for those men to do besides get drunk."

"I don't know what it would be. That's usually the high point of coming to town—getting to the assay office and then the saloon," he answered, not sure where the conversation was leading.

"What if they could come to the restaurant—Maura's and mine—and join us for dinner? Free of charge. We could put Edith in charge of entertainment in case they wanted to stay for a spell after dinner. You know how she loves to see folks have a good time. What do you think?" she asked, an air of excitement overtaking her earlier downcast spirit.

"I'm not sure why you're asking me," he replied. "I think Maura and Edith are the ones you should be talking to."

"But do you at least think it's a good idea?" she persisted.

"It's a real nice idea, Georgette," he conceded.

"And would you be willing to help if we needed you?" she cajoled, once she'd gotten him to admit that her plan was worthy of consideration.

He shook his head and laughed at her.

"You are one insistent woman! You talk to the others, and if they're willing, you can count on me. I'm not sure what I can do, though. My skills in the kitchen leave a lot of room for improvement," he informed her.

"Don't worry. There will be lots of things you can do. I'm going to go and talk to Edith and Maura right away," she told him, walking toward the door.

"By the way, Georgette," he called out, "is there some special reason why you came to extend my dinner invitation instead of Maura?"

She stopped, frozen in her tracks. *Why did he have to ask that?* she thought, not sure how to answer. She wanted to tell the truth, but she certainly didn't want to cause any further breach in the quickly fading marriage of her friend.

"Because Maura asked me to," she simply replied. "I've extended the invitations to all our guests." It was the truth, pure and simple. *Now if I can just get out of here before he questions me any further,* she thought, reaching for the door handle.

"Does she really want me to come?" he questioned, not letting her escape.

"She put your name on the list of guests," Georgette replied, leaving the rest to his imagination. "I really must be going, Luther. If Maura agrees to my idea, we'll need to begin planning right away."

Finally outside, she breathed a sigh of relief. *Maura's not going to put me in that position again,* she resolutely told herself, marching back toward the house.

"What did he say?" Maura inquired the minute Georgette stepped inside the door.

"If I didn't know that you had more important things to do, I'd think you were watching out the window for me," Georgette retorted. "He said he'd be here, but he also wanted to know why I was the one doing the inviting instead of you!"

"What did you tell him?" Maura asked in a shrill voice.

"I told him the truth. Oh, don't panic," she continued, noting the ashen look on her friend's face. "I told him you had placed his name on the list of guests and that I had delivered all of the invitations. Then I rushed out before he could question me any further."

"Thank you, Georgette."

"You're welcome. However, I made up my mind on the way

home that I'm not going to be placed in that position again. It's too uncomfortable, and while I don't want to cause additional problems for you and Luther, I don't want to lie, either. You two are old enough to discuss matters without a go-between," Georgette chided.

"I know that was unfair of me, but I don't think I could have withstood further rejection from him," Maura responded, attempting to assuage her feelings of guilt.

"Forget about it for now. Guess what? While I was inviting Luther, I had the most wonderful idea. Want to hear it?" she asked, enthusiasm replacing the exasperation she'd expressed only minutes earlier.

"Of course! Your ideas are usually quite remarkable," Maura answered, laughing at Georgette's obvious excitement.

"Instead of having a dinner just for the folks we planned on, why don't we invite any of the miners who come into town for Christmas? They'll end up in the saloons trying to drink away their loneliness because there isn't anything else for them to do. What do you think?" she asked, her eyes sparkling in anticipation.

"Oh, Georgette, I don't know. That would be—"

"I know it's a lot of work, but Luther said he'd be willing to help, and you know how Edith loves to entertain. She'd be playing the piano and singing carols—why, she'd probably even have Pastor Wilson give a short sermon. If everyone helps, it won't be that much work, and there probably wouldn't be that many guests," she interrupted, noting the hesitation in Maura's voice.

"It is a generous plan. There's no doubt about that," Maura said, not wanting to deflate Georgette's spirits. "But—"

"Oh, thank you, Maura! I was afraid you would give me a whole list of reasons why we couldn't do it. However, I should have known better, for you don't want all those poor men drinking in a saloon any more than I do," Georgette broke in, obviously fearful of the words that would follow Maura's but.

"Do you realize how little time there is to plan for such a meal?"

"We've already planned it. All we need to do is prepare more," Georgette answered, her smile contagious.

"Have you talked to anyone except Luther about your plan?" Maura asked.

"No—I thought I should talk to you first. But as soon as I feed Becca, I'll go and talk with the others," she answered, her voice filled with anticipation.

"I suppose if they all agree that it's a good idea and they're willing to help, it won't be so difficult. And you're right—it certainly would provide a nice alternative for those men. I do believe you've been blessed with a charitable heart, Georgette," Maura said, amazed at the changes that had taken place in the girl's life since she'd accepted Christ.

## ten

The small group had worked diligently, preparing for the dinner and festivities to be held on Christmas Day. Shortly before midnight on Christmas Eve, Michael arrived to escort Georgette and Becca to midnight services at the small church. Although his invitation included Maura and she knew it was sincere, she once again felt like the extra—"the fifth wheel on the wagon."

*I hate feeling this way. Why can't I just be thankful that I have friends who are willing to include me in their plans instead of resenting my situation?* she thought, removing her woolen cape from the small bedroom closet and pulling a pair of black kid gloves from the dresser drawer. Suddenly, a knock at the front door sent Waffles bounding down the steps in a fit of ferocious barking.

"That dog is going to break his neck flying around the corner and down the steps like that," Maura remarked while coming down the stairway and expecting to see Michael.

"I think he's determined to protect the three of you," Luther replied, grinning. "I stopped to see if I could escort you to Christmas Eve services," he continued with a hint of trepidation in his voice.

"Oh, how nice!" Georgette replied, while clapping her hands together. Noting Maura's stare, she quickly dropped her hands. "I'm sorry. I guess I'm meddling in your business," she said, glancing back and forth between the two of them.

"That's all right. It's good to have someone excited about the invitation," Luther answered.

"Perhaps I'd be more excited had you invited me in advance

112

rather than showing up at the door unexpected," Maura retorted, unable to hold her tongue.

"I'm sorry. I didn't realize that an engraved invitation was necessary to accompany one's spouse to church," he shot back at her.

"Well, I just think it's lovely that the two of you will be spending Christmas Eve together in God's house," Georgette interjected.

The two of them turned toward her simultaneously.

"Who asked you?" they questioned in unison, their faces contorted in anger.

Forlornly, she gazed at them. A tear slid down her cheek. "I wish you could see yourselves. If so, perhaps you'd have a change of heart," she replied before walking away from them and back toward her bedroom.

"Georgette!" Maura called, following behind the girl. She could feel Luther's stare as she limped into the parlor. Glancing over her shoulder, she saw him watching her.

"Is that pity or disgust?" she asked in a razor-thin voice.

"Neither—it's astonishment. Astonishment at how something that seemed so right could turn out so wrong," he replied, shaking his head as he walked out the door.

"Georgette, let me explain," Maura began as she entered her friend's bedroom. Before she could go any further, another knock sounded at the door.

"I'll get it," Maura said when Georgette began to stand up. "I'm sure it's Luther returning to apologize."

Waffles ran along beside her as she entered the front hallway and opened the door. "Merry Christmas," Michael greeted. "Everyone ready to go?"

"Just about," Maura replied, attempting to hide her disappointment. She had been certain that it would be Luther. *I should have known better,* she thought as her disappointment gave way to anger.

"It's Michael," she announced, walking into the bedroom.

"I should have known that Luther wouldn't return," she indignantly announced to Georgette.

"Why should he? And why should you want him to?" Georgette asked, bewildered by Maura's behavior. "I'd think you would have had enough dissension for one evening. Personally, I'd like to go to church without any further upheavals. Are you going to join us or not?"

"Yes," Maura replied, feeling the sting of Georgette's reproach. "I apologize for my undignified conduct. I don't want to spoil your holiday."

"You don't owe me an apology, Maura, and it's not the holiday I'm concerned about. It's you—you and Luther and—"

"We're keeping Michael waiting," Maura interrupted, knowing that further discussion would only lead to more words spoken in anger—words that couldn't be taken back.

The services were just beginning as they entered the church and slipped in a pew near the back of the church. The candles at the front of the church offered only a dim glow, which made it impossible for Maura to spot Luther.

*He probably went home,* she thought, leaning toward Georgette in an attempt to gain a better view.

"Don't you have enough room?" Georgette whispered, scooting a bit closer to Michael.

"Yes," Maura answered. Hoping Georgette didn't realize that she had been looking for Luther, she forced herself to keep her eyes focused on Pastor Wilson throughout the remainder of the sermon.

As Edith struck the opening chords of "O Little Town of Bethlehem," their individual candles were lit, filling the church with a shadowy, flickering light that trailed out into the night as they left for their homes.

"Do you still want me to help tomorrow?"

Maura turned, startled to see Luther standing behind her. "I thought you'd gone home," she replied.

"No, I was sitting up front. Would it be better if I didn't

come tomorrow? I'll do whatever you want. I don't want to be the cause of ruining all the hard work that's gone into your dinner plans."

"Of course we want you to come! Besides, we need your help," Georgette answered before Maura could say a word. "I think we're going to need every pair of hands we can get! At least that's my opinion," she finished, looking toward Maura.

"I agree. We'll need all the help we can get," she replied.

"In that case, I'll plan to be there. Good night to all of you," he said, his look encompassing the three of them.

"I'll be down early in the morning to help you carry that lumber up to the house," Michael responded. "Good night!"

Luther waved his hand in reply and continued walking toward the store, with a bit of a slump to his shoulders and slowness to his stride.

The three of them walked home in silence; even Becca remained silent, the cold air apparently not disturbing her sleep. When they reached the house, Maura extended her arms to take the baby from Georgette.

"I'll put her to bed. You two go ahead and say your good nights," she offered.

"Thank you," Georgette whispered as she handed her the baby.

Becca was soon snuggled into her cradle beside Georgette's bed. Giving the baby one last kiss, Maura returned to the parlor.

"You two appear to be deep in conversation. However, I was going to retire for the night. It's late, and we'll have to begin preparations early tomorrow," Maura said in an obvious attempt to speed Michael's departure.

"There's no need for you to wait up. We had a few matters to discuss, but we're almost through. Michael will be leaving momentarily," Georgette explained, giving her friend a smile. "Good night, Maura," the couple called out as she walked toward the stairway.

"Good night," she whispered as a lump began to rise in her throat.

*Why am I feeling sorry for myself? I could be sitting downstairs holding hands with Luther or living under the same roof if I chose,* she thought as she began to undress for bed. *Then why do I feel so miserable, and why am I so jealous of anyone else who has a relationship?* she questioned herself. Slowly she unpinned and brushed her long auburn hair, stroke after stroke, until her arm began to ache.

*You need some changes in your heart,* a small voice whispered inside her head. Shocked at the revelation, Maura sat looking in the mirror.

"I need to change. Me! It's always me that's wrong; it's always me that must give in and overlook the way others treat me," she murmured aloud. "That's not fair. Why doesn't anybody else need to change?"

*Me, me, me. Poor me,* came the small voice once again. *You can either change your heart or turn into a bitter old woman, unloved and wallowing in self-pity. Luther will meet you part way, if you'll only give him a chance. It might help to have a positive approach instead of your usual negative attitude when you're around him,* the nagging voice continued in her thoughts.

Slowly Maura walked to the bed and got down on her knees. "Is that You talking to me, God?" she whispered, a trickle of tears escaping her eyes "I know you're right—that I've become bitter through the years. Even more so since marrying Luther. I wanted to have a good marriage—like Daniel and Amanda's—is that so much to ask?"

There was no answer—only the stillness of the cold starry night. "I'll try, God. If that's what You want, I'll try," she promised, rising from her knees.

❧

Morning arrived all too quickly, and Maura awakened to the sounds of Michael's and Luther's voices, mixed with Waffles's occasional barking.

"I've overslept," she scolded herself, yet she wanted to remain under the warm covers.

"Maura, are you up?" came Georgette's voice calling up the stairs.

"I overslept. I'll be down shortly," she replied, hurrying to make herself presentable.

"That's a first," Georgette commented to Michael.

"What's that?"

"Maura oversleeping. I've never known her to do that," she answered.

"She was probably exhausted from all the trouble she caused Luther yesterday," Michael retorted.

"Michael! If that was the case, they'd both have overslept because Luther was dishing it out just as fast as Maura," she half-mockingly scolded him.

"What are you two talking about? Thought I heard my name mentioned," Luther remarked. "You want to help me with that lumber?" he continued, not waiting for an answer to his previous question.

"Think we ought to get the makeshift tables and benches set up?" Michael asked Georgette.

"Why don't you just carry the lumber up here, and we'll wait until we need them? There are quite a few tables and chairs in the dining area already, and I'm not sure how many men will actually show up. Besides, it will save having to fight our way around all that extra 'furniture' until closer to dinner time," she suggested.

"Sounds fine with me," Luther answered. "We'll just load it into the wagon and bring it over here. No need to unload it unless there's a need," he advised Michael as the two walked toward Luther's store.

Luther led Michael to the storage barn behind the store, and the two of them chose pieces of lumber to place in the wagon. "We'll take those wider ones to use for tables; the narrower ones will make good benches," Luther advised. "I think we can use those smaller barrels under the benches, and I've got lots of the big ones to use under the tables."

"How many you think we'll need?" Michael inquired.

"Don't have any idea, but even with rearranging, that dining room is only going to hold two of these setups. If there are too many guests, either they'll have to wait their turn or, if it's not too cold, we'll see if Maura and Georgette want to put a couple tables outside," Luther replied.

When they'd finished loading all the necessary items for the makeshift seating, they hitched up the team and led the horses up the street and to the rear of the restaurant. Once the horses had come to a complete halt, Luther deftly unhitched the team and walked them back around to the front of the house.

"I'm going to take the horses back down to my barn. No sense in having them hitched up here all day," he told Michael.

"Good morning, Luther," Maura called out, walking onto the front porch.

"Mornin' and Merry Christmas to you," Luther tentatively answered.

"You want some company walking the horses back?" she offered.

"I can take 'em—unless you're anxious for some exercise," he added.

"I'll probably get all the exercise I need today fixing and serving dinner, but I wouldn't mind the company," she said, giving him a cheery smile and joining him at the bottom of the steps.

"In that case, come along," he replied, giving her a half-hearted smile in return. "You know, Maura, you're a hard person to figure out. Last night you were so angry that I didn't know if you wanted me to come over here and help out today. And now, this morning, you act like there's nothing you enjoy more than being in my company. Am I dense or missing something here? To be quite honest, I just don't understand you," he remarked as they walked alongside the horses.

She shook her head in acknowledgment of his statement but took the time to carefully form her thoughts before answering.

"I'm sure you don't—and I'm not sure I understand you, either. But if we're ever going to begin understanding one another, I think we need to call a truce. That's why I wanted to be alone with you for a few minutes," she told him as they walked into the barn.

Watching as Luther uncinched the gray dapple work-horses, Maura fidgeted when he did not immediately reply. He began to remove the horses' leather collars and, when he had finished, he walked over and positioned himself behind the railing surrounding the stall where she stood. Resting his arms on the top strip of wood and allowing his upper body to lean forward, he whispered, "What kind of truce did you have in mind?"

As he spoke, she could feel his warm breath on her neck. It sent shivers running up and down her spine, and she felt her cheeks turning hot. Her mind raced back to their wedding day and the passionate kiss Luther had placed upon her lips. Unconsciously, she traced a finger across her mouth. Not wanting him to know the effect he was having upon her, she dared not move.

"I thought perhaps we could try speaking to and treating each other more kindly," she weakly ventured, unsure exactly what to propose.

"Is that all you thought?" he asked, once again leaning close to her neck before he spoke.

"No, but it's a starting place," she replied.

He moved from behind her and walked around the stall, placing himself directly in front of her. Carefully, he placed his hands on either side of her waist and lifted her onto one of the tall barrels sitting close by. She didn't resist but gave him a questioning look.

"I want to see your eyes when you talk to me," he said in answer to her look. "Instead of all those vague answers you've given me, why don't you tell me what you really want—from me, from this so-called marriage, from life itself."

Maura wriggled uncomfortably. She hadn't anticipated being placed in a position in which she might have to reveal her inner thoughts to him.

"I'm not sure we have time now for such a deep conversation. I need to assist with dinner preparations. Besides, everyone will be wondering where we are," she ventured, hoping to escape his pointed questions. She needed time for thoughtful introspection before she answered—time to carefully prepare.

"There are enough folks in that kitchen that they'll be falling all over each other. Besides, I told Michael we might be gone for a while. He'll be able to answer any questions that might arise regarding our whereabouts. Since we are married, there's certainly no need to worry about any impropriety in our being alone, is there?" he asked, already knowing the answer.

"Well, no. . ." she haltingly replied.

"So tell me, Maura Buchanan, what is it you want?" he once again asked.

Maura Buchanan. The name sounded foreign to her ears. She still thought of herself as Maura Thorenson.

"When you think of yourself, you think of Maura Thorenson—not Maura Buchanan. Am I right?" he asked, when she hadn't replied to his earlier question.

Her head snapped up at his remark. How did he know what she was thinking? There was a twinkle in his inquiring mahogany eyes.

"It makes you uncomfortable that I could have any idea of what you're thinking, doesn't it?"

Before she could reply, he bent his head and pulled her to him, his full lips gently caressing hers and then quickly giving way to the urgency of his passion—a passion he had held in reserve throughout these months of marriage. She responded, leaning forward and placing her arms around his neck, her breath shallow as his lips explored hers with an unrelenting hunger.

"You were thinking of that, too, weren't you?" he whispered, when their lips finally parted.

Fearing that she would slip off the barrel if he released her, she leaned back against the railing, her body gone limp from the intensity of their mutual ardor.

"Yes," she honestly answered.

"And what else were you thinking?" he urged.

"I want a devoted husband who is affectionate and tender. A husband who will allow me to share his life, who admires my strengths and overlooks my imperfections. I want a husband who loves God and wants the kind of marriage God intended for His children," she candidly replied, Luther's kiss having erased her fears. "I usually hide my true feelings for I'm not as vulnerable if people don't know what I really feel," she explained.

He smiled at her, tenderly lifted a strand of hair, and then tucked it behind her ear. "The problem with hiding your true feelings from your marriage partner is that you never receive the full joy God intended. I realize that being honest makes you more susceptible to being hurt. But when you are open and honest with the person you love, it gives him the opportunity to fulfill your expectations instead of leaving that person merely to guess how to please you."

She nodded her head but wasn't sure she was willing to go quite that far.

"For instance, there is nothing improper about a wife telling her husband she would like to be kissed. You see, husbands don't automatically know those things," he instructed.

"I would like that," she said, lifting her head and closing her eyes.

He broke forth in a laugh and then stopped himself when he saw the pained look she gave him. Quickly, he leaned down to kiss her, only to be rebuffed.

"Maura, you misinterpreted my laughter," he admonished when she turned her head as he once again attempted to kiss her. "You can't always assume the worst when people laugh. I am pleased that you want me to kiss you. Truly, I am. I laughed only because I was using the statement about kissing as an illustration and you took it literally. I'll try to be more careful in the future if you'll try to be less sensitive," he suggested.

She glanced up at him and saw a look of pleading in his eyes.

"I think I would still like a kiss," she said, breaking the uncomfortable silence. This time he didn't laugh as he gathered her into his arms.

"We have a lot more to talk about," he said, once he'd released her from his embrace, "but I suppose we should get back to the house."

Maura gathered her shawl as they walked from the barn.

"I believe it's getting cooler," Luther remarked, taking the shawl and placing it around her shoulders.

Maura nodded in affirmation. "I think I'd like for you to keep your arm around my shoulder," she said, smiling.

"I think I'd like that, too," he replied, placing his arm around her shoulder and pulling her close while they made their way down the street.

## eleven

"Maura! Where have you been?" Georgette scolded as the couple walked into the house.

"Luther and I returned his horses to the barn," she replied, smiling when Luther winked at her.

"Well, don't just stand there. We'll have guests arriving soon, and the rest of us have been hard at work while you've been gone. You should have been here helping," she continued.

"She was exactly where she needed to be, Georgette," Luther replied. "Please don't be harsh with Maura. It's really my fault for keeping her away, but there were things we needed to discuss. Things I felt were more important to our future than the dinner. She wanted to return, but I assured her there were plenty of hands to prepare the meal," he defended, his voice protective.

Georgette gave him a stunned look and then shifted her eyes back toward Maura. "So you two have been talking," she remarked, seeing the look on her friend's face. "In that case, how could I object? Did this talking have an amiable outcome?" she asked.

"I would say it did. Wouldn't you agree, Luther?" Maura inquired, looking at him, wishing she could ask for another kiss.

"Most amiable, although we didn't have enough time to resolve all of the issues we wanted to discuss. Did we, my dear?" he asked, giving her a light kiss.

"No, not everything," she agreed, realizing he had once again known what she was thinking. It was most disconcerting. She'd have to be careful what she thought!

Georgette stood momentarily transfixed. Was this the same

bickering couple that she'd been with only last night? "God certainly can work miracles," she murmured, walking toward the kitchen.

"You go and help her, my sweet, and I'll see what I can do to help Michael," Luther said, leaning down to kiss her cheek.

*My sweet, he called me "my sweet,"* she thought, walking into the kitchen. However, it didn't take long for the culinary mayhem to push all thoughts of Luther from her mind. Surveying the situation, it became immediately obvious that no one had taken time to organize the group of women. Everyone was scurrying about, but not much was being accomplished.

"Ladies!" Maura called out, quickly gaining their attention. "It appears that we need a bit of teamwork if we're to prepare and serve this meal on time. I think the easiest plan would be to make assignments. Is that all right with all of you?" she asked, though not waiting for an answer. "Georgette, you're in charge of the meat; have Michael help you with carving when you're ready. Edith, you're in charge of the stuffing and sweet potatoes—"

"But the turkeys have already been stuffed. Don't you want me to do something besides the sweet potatoes?" the excited parson's wife asked.

"You can prepare the mashed potatoes also, but remember you'll need to help Georgette unstuff those turkeys when they're ready," Maura answered, giving Edith a smile.

And so it went. Maura assigned the tasks and each of the women was responsible from beginning to end for those particular foods or tasks. Earlier they had placed signs about town informing folks of the dinner, but Maura thought it would be a nice gesture to personally invite folks so that they would feel genuinely welcome. To that end, she went seeking her husband.

"Luther, there you are," she said, walking into the parlor

where Michael and Luther were tending Becca. "Don't you think it would be hospitable to go to the saloons and gaming parlors and invite the men to dinner? They may not see the signs; besides, some of them may not be able to read."

Luther leaned back in the sturdy oak chair, balancing on the back two legs and holding himself steady with the tips of his toes resting on the floor in front of him. He gave her a slow grin.

"Maura, my dear wife, do you have any idea how the owners of those saloons and gambling halls are going to react when I walk in and invite their customers to leave for a free meal?"

She shook her head and waited.

"They are going to be very unhappy. This is one of the busiest times of year for them. In fact, the men spend most of their money trying to drown or forget their loneliness during this time of year," he carefully explained.

"Well, I know that, Luther. That's why we planned this get-together!" Maura replied, with exasperation written on her face. "I thought you were going to reveal some really good reason why you couldn't go invite folks."

He stared at her and then looked at Michael for assistance.

"Go ahead, Luther. You're doing fine. Explain it to her," Michael said, while trying to hide the smirk on his face.

"Let me put it this way, my dear. If I go into those businesses and ask the customers to leave and come over here for free food and festivities, the owners of those businesses may never speak to me again. They're going to be angry because we'll be the cause of their losing money," he politely explained in a measured tone of voice.

"Well, if that's the only problem, invite them, too. We'd be happy to have them join us," she answered, giving him a sweet smile while totally dismissing the portion of his answer relating to the lost business of the local merchants.

"I think perhaps those who want to attend will come without

a special invitation," Luther said in a feeble attempt to side-step the whole issue.

"If you don't want to go, I'm sure that Michael would be willing to assist," Maura replied, giving him a stern look and turning toward new prey for her holiday mission.

"You know I would do that for you, Maura, but Georgette told me that I dare not leave this parlor. She said she'd be more than a little upset if she came looking for me to help carve the meat and I wasn't around," he replied, clearly pleased at how adroitly he had avoided the trap.

"I see," Maura replied. Saying nothing further, she walked back toward the kitchen as the two men looked at each other and sighed with relief.

It had been only a few minutes when they saw her returning with Amelia Bergman in tow. "Amelia is going to tend Becca for the rest of the afternoon," she advised them, taking the baby from Michael and placing her in Amelia's capable arms.

"You sure she's old enough to look after a baby?" Michael asked, a sense of foreboding in his voice.

"Of course, she is. She's fifteen years old and has seven younger brothers and sisters. She's had loads of experience, haven't you, Amelia?" she asked the young girl.

Amelia nodded her head in affirmation and walked toward the bedroom carrying her young charge.

"Now, then, gentlemen, I think we've been able to work out a plan," Maura announced as the two men looked at each other with trepidation.

Looking at Luther, she said in her sweetest voice, "I am doing as you requested earlier, Luther. I'm being open and honest with you in order to allow you the opportunity to fulfill my expectations."

"This isn't quite what I had in mind when we talked. . ." Luther began.

"Well, we never know when an opportunity will present

itself, do we? In any event, it would make me extremely happy if you and Michael would go and extend a personal invitation around town," she said in an agreeable tone.

"But—" Michael began.

"Georgette said she wouldn't need you for at least an hour, Michael," she interrupted before the young man could protest being included.

The two men exchanged a look of doom. "Guess we'd just as well get this over with, Michael," Luther said as he rose from the chair. Maura followed behind them as they walked onto the porch and down the steps.

"Luther," she called just as the men reached the bottom of the stairs.

He turned and walked back toward her. "When you return, I think I would like a kiss," she said, giving him a captivating smile.

"I'll be happy to meet that expectation," he said, laughing as he caught up with Michael.

Almost an hour had passed when Michael and Luther returned to the house, and Georgette quickly rushed Michael into the kitchen to assist her with the turkeys. Spying Michael as he began to carve one of the birds, Maura walked into the parlor.

"I see that you're back all in one piece," she said to Luther, smiling.

Without a word, he swept her into his arms and kissed her soundly, which left her breathless as he slowly pulled away from her.

"I am all in one piece, my dear, but just remember that you are the one who sent me out extending invitations," he said, causing her to wonder at the remark.

"Did the business owners become angry?" she inquired.

"They weren't overly pleased, but I guess they'll get over it," he answered. "By the way, how many did you say you'd planned on serving?"

"I'm not sure, but I think we'll have plenty of food. Why do you ask?" she inquired.

He didn't answer but merely pointed his finger down the street toward a throng of people headed toward the house. Her eyes grew wide as she looked from the street toward Luther and then back again.

"Are they all coming here?" Maura inquired.

"Yep!"

"All of them?" she asked, incredulously.

"All of them. After Michael and I had visited a couple of the saloons, the owners got together and decided that the best thing to do was just close down and let their employees as well as their patrons attend your dinner. You're going to feed everyone from the miners to the dance hall girls," he told her.

"This is more than I expected, and I know it's more than Georgette expected," she replied, with a note of fear in her voice.

He turned toward her and smiled. "Like you said earlier, you never know when an opportunity will present itself. Just look at this as an opportunity, Maura. In fact, you may never get another chance to minister to this many unsaved folks at one time."

"But there are so many," she said, as the crowd grew closer.

"Hopefully those turkeys and hams will stretch as far as the loaves and fishes," he said, placing a protective arm around her. "We'll manage," he said in a comforting voice when she gave him a doleful look.

Maura returned to the kitchen as fast as her legs would allow, though her left hip and leg had begun to ache. She'd been on her feet all day, and her limp always worsened when she began to tire.

"Georgette," she called in a loud whisper. "Our guests are arriving. Many more than we anticipated," she said, looking at her friend.

"I know. Michael told me. What are we going to do?"

"We'll just have to organize ourselves. I think if we set up a line and have them come through with their plates, not only can we control the portion sizes, but also it may control seating. By the time the ones at the beginning of the line are done eating, they can free their places for the others. If we run out of food, we'll apologize and let them know we'll plan for more guests next year," she said with a shrug.

Hastily issuing instructions to the men and women assisting, Maura gave the dining room one last glance. It was chilly, but at least the weather was bearable. At the last moment Maura asked Michael and Luther to move the small piano onto the front porch so that Edith could play Christmas carols. If anyone could keep a group in good humor, it was Edith.

Assuring Maura she was up to the challenge, Edith delightedly took her place at the piano. Before long, the strains of "Silent Night" being sung by the crowd filled the house, and soon the dinner was being served to the crowd.

Maura's plan worked. Their guests didn't seem to mind the wait once they reached the kitchen and were served the finely prepared meal. The biggest problem turned out to be keeping enough clean dishes; however, once again Maura convinced Luther and Michael to aid the women who were rushing to wash, dry, and replace the plates, cups, and silverware. They helped with the chore until several of the dance hall girls asked if they could assist. Maura quickly accepted their offer and put the men to work at other chores.

After all of the guests had been served, the kitchen cleaned, and the rest of the group had departed, Maura, Luther, Georgette, and Michael sat down in the parlor before the glowing fire Michael had started a few hours earlier.

Luther and Maura were seated on the tapestry-covered loveseat. His arm was draped around her shoulders and her head rested against his arm. Michael and Georgette were deep in conversation regarding the events of the day when

Luther leaned down and kissed Maura's ear.

She looked up and smiled sleepily.

"Come home with me?" he asked.

"I am home, Luther," she replied but felt him stiffen as soon as she said the words.

"Your home is with me," he rebutted, keeping his voice low.

"Well, yes, that's true enough. But, Georgette and I bought this place. You know that. I can't just walk off and leave her alone," she whispered.

"Would you like for us to leave you alone?" Michael asked.

"No," Maura said.

"Yes, that would be appreciated," Luther replied, overriding her answer.

As soon as they'd left the room, Luther turned toward Maura. "I want you to come home and begin our life as husband and wife, Maura. We've begun to work out our problems, and we need to be together if we're going to make our marriage succeed," he told her.

"I know there is truth in what you're saying, but there is so much left for us to discuss and, as I said a few minutes ago, I can't just walk out on Georgette."

"You didn't seem to have much problem walking out on me," he reminded her, trying to remain patient.

"You've told me to be honest and open with you. I'm going to try and do that, Luther, and I hope I won't regret it," she said, turning to look at him and taking his hand in hers. "I believe it would be best if we at least discuss our problems and how we can resolve them before I return. I won't deny my feelings for you—I'm sure you've already guessed how much I care for you, but I won't deny that you've hurt me deeply also. I don't want that to happen again. Let's take a little time and do this right," she pleaded.

"Just because we wait six months or six years doesn't assure we'll be happy," he said, obviously referring to the six-month waiting period she'd invoked prior to their marriage.

"I'm not talking about six months, Luther. Just enough time to discuss some of the problems we face and how to resolve them. And whether or not you want to acknowledge it, leaving Georgette and the baby living alone is different from when I left you. She'd have to find someone to stay at the house with her, at least during the night. She'd be scared to death to stay alone, and after what happened to me, I certainly wouldn't want to place her in such a precarious position. Of course, I'd be there during the day to help her with the restaurant," she continued.

"You plan to continue the restaurant venture? Even after you return home? I don't think that would ever work," he said incredulously.

"You see, Luther, there are many things for us to resolve. I want our marriage to succeed, probably more than you can imagine. But it would be folly for me to return now," she told him.

"Then I suppose there's nothing left to say," he answered, rising to leave.

"That's just it, Luther—there is everything left to say," she replied. "Please tell me that you're not angry and that we'll talk further," she implored.

"You've misunderstood me again, my dear. I merely meant there was nothing further to say about your returning home tonight. We will talk and we will resolve our differences and you will return home," he stated, his voice filled with confidence.

"You sound very sure of yourself," she replied.

"I'm sure of God's plan for us, and I'm sure that I love you, Maura Buchanan," he told her, holding out his hand to her.

She rose to meet his waiting arms and feel the warmth of his kiss. They walked toward the front door and, after they kissed good night, she watched him as he walked down the street. Surprising her, he turned, blew her a kiss, and called out, "Merry Christmas."

"Merry Christmas," she called back. *You're a complex man, Luther Buchanan,* she thought, just as Michael and Georgette walked outside.

"Luther gone home for the night?" Michael asked.

"Yes, for the night," Maura answered and then returned indoors, leaving the couple to say their good nights.

# twelve

Maura rose early the next morning and had finished preparing breakfast before Georgette awakened.

"Aren't you the early bird," Georgette said, walking into the kitchen. "You ought to enjoy these last few days before we open the restaurant—sleep in while you can," she said, giving her friend a charming smile. "Are you planning on serving breakfast to the whole town or are you extra hungry?" Georgette continued, eyeing the plates of ham, eggs, biscuits, and gravy.

"I thought I'd take Luther's breakfast down to him," Maura replied, avoiding Georgette's watchful gaze.

"That's a first, isn't it?" Georgette inquired. "It appears that the two of you are getting things worked out. It was nice to see you snuggled together last evening—just like a married couple should be," she continued, not waiting for an answer to her question.

"Luther has told me that he wants the marriage to work and that he cares for me," she told her friend. "I believe him, but we need to resolve some of our differences before we make another attempt at living together."

"Living together! I hadn't given any thought to that. When the two of you get your problems resolved, I'll be left alone," Georgette said, a slight sound of panic in her voice.

"Please don't worry, Georgette. I won't leave before we make suitable living arrangements," Maura reassured her friend.

"You're not going to desert me, are you? And what about our business? I can't do this on my own, Maura. I need you," she pleaded, fear evident in her eyes.

"Georgette, please don't cry," Maura said, enveloping her friend and hugging her close. "We'll work this out. I promise—and I take my promises seriously," she said. "Now, you go get ready for the day, and I'll take this food down to Luther and be back shortly."

The bell over the door announced Maura's entrance, although Luther knew she was coming. He'd seen her leaving the house and watched as she walked down the street, carrying a basket over her arm. His heart gave a small leap of pleasure when she cheerfully announced that she'd brought him breakfast.

"Did I arrive in time, or have you already had breakfast?" she asked, handing him the wicker basket.

"I haven't eaten yet, but even if I had, there'd still be room for your cooking," he praised, enjoying the blush it brought to her cheeks.

Removing the contents of the basket, he gestured toward a chair. "Please sit down and visit with me," he offered.

"I told Georgette I'd be right back," she said. "When she saw that I had fixed breakfast for you, the realization that we might get back together hit her. Don't misunderstand—she wants nothing more than for us to be reunited—but she's fearful of her future. I promised her I wouldn't move out until we'd agreed upon satisfactory arrangements," she continued.

"That could take a long time, Maura. Perhaps you shouldn't have made such a promise," he cautioned.

"The Lord will provide a way when the time is right. I'm sure of it," she told him. "Is there a time today when we could talk further?" she asked invitingly.

"Why don't you come here? That way Georgette won't feel that she's confined to her room while we're talking," he answered. "As soon as I've closed the store, I'll come and fetch you."

"Come for supper, and we can leave after that," she suggested.

"That sounds good," he answered, obviously pleased that she wanted to continue their conversation.

"I'd better be getting back. Just bring those along when you come," she instructed, indicating the dishes and basket.

"I'll do that. Thank you for breakfast. It's delicious," he said, dipping one of the biscuits into the creamy white gravy.

"You are most welcome," she graciously replied as she left the store.

Maura had just begun walking toward home when she saw Edith rushing toward her and waving her arm. "Maura! Maura!" the woman called out.

"What is it, Edith? Is something wrong with Georgette?" she asked, fearful for her friend and the baby.

"No, no, they're fine. I stopped by to see you, and Georgette said you were at the store with Luther. She said to tell you she was taking Becca for some fresh air. Do you have time for a visit?"

"Certainly. Come back to the house, and I'll fix a fresh pot of coffee," she suggested.

Removing the china cups and flowered china dishes from the walnut cabinet in the dining room, Maura carried them into the kitchen and poured the steaming liquid into the two cups. She carefully arranged some biscuits on one of the plates and placed it in the center of the table alongside a small crock of strawberry preserves.

"What brings you visiting so early this morning?" Maura asked as she settled in the chair opposite her visitor.

"You'll be so pleased to hear my news—I just couldn't wait to come tell you," Edith chortled. "After Charles and I returned home last night, we had a visitor."

She said nothing further, and Maura knew that she was expected to encourage her. "And who was that?" she asked, playing along.

"One of the dance hall girls, the one with the black curls.

Her name is Marie McTavish," Edith told her. "She said you visited with her for a short time while she was washing dishes."

"Yes, I remember her," Maura recalled. "A pretty girl. She asked me several questions about why we were hosting the dinner. When I told her we wanted to give folks an option other than gambling or drinking to celebrate Christ's birth, she seemed genuinely touched. However, I didn't have time to visit very long, and when I returned later, she was gone."

"Well, she came to our house last night at about nine o'clock. Said she wanted to ask some questions about being a Christian. Charles was so good with her, explaining things carefully. He revealed the plan of salvation and then read to her from Romans 10:9-13. She became so excited when Charles assured her that God would forgive her sins. It truly brought tears to my eyes hearing her. When I was listening to her talk, it was apparent that the poor girl thought no one else in the world had ever been as sinful as she had been. After several hours of talking and praying, she accepted Christ as her Savior. Can you believe it? God gave us a miracle yesterday!" she exclaimed.

"I think He probably gave us more than one," Maura replied, "but that is certainly wonderful news. I'm sure that the angels are rejoicing for Marie, and I'm happy that you came and shared the information with me."

Edith gave Maura a timid smile. "It's true that I wanted you to hear the news right away, but there's a little more we need to talk about," she said, a note of reticence in her voice.

"What's that?" Maura inquired, not sure where the conversation was leading.

"Needless to say, Marie doesn't want to return to her previous lifestyle and, well, I don't think she'd be happy staying with Charles and me. Besides, I'm not sure that the parishioners would agree to that type of arrangement on a long-term basis. So, after I went to bed last night, a thought came to mind that perhaps. . ."

Edith left the sentence dangling while she took a sip of coffee.

When Maura said nothing, she finally asked, "Well, what do you think?"

"About what, Edith? You said that a thought came to mind, but you didn't tell me what it was," Maura answered.

"Well, I was hoping for an invitation for Marie to move in here with you and Georgette," she replied, giving Maura a look of exasperation. "You're such a bright young lady, Maura, that I was sure you'd know what plan came to my mind."

"You can't be serious, Edith! We don't even know her," Maura exclaimed.

"Know who?" Georgette inquired, catching the tail end of the conversation as she entered the house with Becca in her arms.

"Marie McTavish. She's one of the dance hall girls that attended the dinner—" Edith began.

"She was converted last night, and now Edith has come to ask if she can move in with us," Maura interrupted.

"Move in with us?" Georgette asked, a look of shock on her face. "A dance hall girl?"

"A converted dance hall girl," Edith corrected.

"Good heavens, Edith, I don't know how you could even ask such a thing. I have a young daughter to rear, and I certainly don't need the influence of a woman of ill repute living with us," Georgette replied, giving the older woman a stern look.

"'Let he who is without sin cast the first stone,'" Edith quietly responded. "This young lady has accepted Jesus Christ as her Lord and Savior. She needs the support and affection of Christians, not judgment and derision. However, I've obviously made an error in judgment. Please forgive me," she said as she rose from her chair.

"Wait, Edith," Maura said, taking the woman's hand. "You must realize the fact that you've caught us completely off guard with your request. I'm not saying it's totally out of the question, but Georgette and I really need to discuss this. Why don't you come back after lunch, and we'll talk further?" she requested.

"I'll be happy to do that," she answered somewhat dejectedly, her spirit of enthusiasm waning.

No sooner had she left the house than Georgette turned on Maura. "How can you even consider such a thing? She's an immoral woman. What kind of message would we be sending to the community if we harbored the likes of her?"

"Listen to yourself, Georgette. Christ forgave you when you became a Christian, He forgave me when I became a Christian, and He forgave Marie when she became a Christian. Who she was and how she supported herself in the past has no bearing on the conversation at hand."

"Oh, really?" Georgette questioned sarcastically.

"I seem to recall you repeating a certain statement to me a while back. It was a comment I'd made to you about Christians being so unforgiving and critical of each other that Satan can just sit around and enjoy the chaos that they create for each other. Do you remember that?" Maura inquired.

"Yes, I remember that. But we were talking about you and Luther. It was a totally different set of circumstances."

"I see," Maura replied. "So you think we should be able to pick and choose the circumstances to which we apply God's principles?"

"Well, not exactly, but I think this is different," Georgette stubbornly answered.

"I don't want to hurt you, Georgette, but please tell me how you rationalize your decision. You needed refuge and assistance when you were pregnant with an illegitimate child. I felt it was my Christian responsibility to help you, and God has blessed me with a wonderful friend because of the assistance I rendered to you and Becca. How can you now so quickly dismiss another woman in need?" Maura asked.

"You make me sound like a wretch," she said in a hushed voice. "Deep down I know that we should help her, but I'm so afraid of bringing unwanted attention upon myself or Becca. I don't want people to find out about the circumstances of her birth. In fact, I haven't even told Michael. You and Luther are the only ones that know, and I live in daily fear that he'll tell Michael. I know that it's selfishness on my part, because I don't want to face the ugliness in my past."

Without a word, Maura placed her arm around Georgette's shoulder and gave her a reassuring hug.

"We all have things in our past that we're ashamed of, but we can't let that be a deterrent to helping others. Satan uses that old scheme a lot," she reminded Georgette.

"I know what you say is right, but I don't want things to change," Georgette replied, her voice barely audible.

"Life is full of continual changes, Georgette. Nothing stays the same. Besides, most changes are exciting and fun if we keep an open mind about what God has planned for us."

"What's fun about all of this?" she asked, pursing her lips in a pout.

"Maybe I should rephrase that. Sometimes changes are exciting and fun—other times they may be painful. What I do know is that God always leaves us with a message through those changes, and those messages are exciting," she explained.

"I suppose it wouldn't hurt to talk to her. If we do agree, where is she going to stay? The only furnished bedrooms are yours and mine," Georgette reminded Maura.

"I think that Charles and Edith would be willing to have her remain with them for a short time, at least until we can make adequate arrangements for furniture. Edith's concern was that Marie have some type of permanent living arrangement in place, not that she move her out immediately."

"If that's the case, perhaps we could ask Michael about making a bed," Georgette suggested.

Maura smiled at Georgette, who had gone from one extreme to the other in a matter of minutes. First she had wanted nothing to do with Marie, but now she had Michael making a brand new bed.

"Why don't we meet with Marie? If we find her personality agreeable, perhaps she could come over during the days and help us get ready for the opening of the restaurant. If we all get along and it appears that we could live together, we'll make plans for furnishing a bedroom. What do you think?" Maura asked.

"That sounds reasonable. We can certainly use her help with the restaurant—if she has any talent in that direction. I'm sorry. That was an unkind remark," Georgette quickly added, a blush rising in her cheeks.

"Well, we already know that she can wash dishes," Maura replied. "That's a beginning."

Edith returned several hours later, her typically bubbly personality obviously heightened by the answer that she now anticipated receiving. She fluttered into the house and never ceased talking until Georgette placed a cup of tea and plate of cookies in front of her.

"Oh, thank you, my dear," she said, taking a bite of an applesauce cookie. "These are wonderful," she continued, wiping the corners of her mouth with the linen napkin Georgette had supplied.

"Why don't you enjoy your tea, and I'll tell you the plan we have in mind," Maura suggested, as Edith took another bite of cookie.

The older woman nodded her head in agreement as she sipped the cup of tea.

"Since we have only the two bedrooms furnished—" Maura began.

"Oh, well, we can—" Edith interrupted.

"Edith! Please allow me to finish explaining; then you may add your comments," Maura admonished firmly.

"I'm sorry," Edith answered meekly, her effervescent nature clearly hard to control at times.

"As I was saying, since we have only two bedrooms furnished, Georgette and I thought that Marie could come here to work alongside us, preparing for the opening of the restaurant during the day. Then at night, she would return to stay with you and Charles. During this time of becoming acquainted, we would see about furnishing one of the other upstairs bedrooms. If we find ourselves harmonious—and we will make every attempt to do so—we will then offer Marie a home with us. What do you think?" Maura questioned.

Edith had lost some of her earlier animation and sat quietly for a moment as she finished the last of her tea.

"I don't suppose there is much choice, if that's what you think best. I had hoped you would welcome her immediately," Edith replied, with a lingering note of persuasiveness in her voice.

"Now, Edith, don't try to make us feel guilty. We've already had a discussion about guilt earlier this morning. I think our decision will prove best for all three of us. If we find that we're incompatible, it will be kinder to Marie if she hasn't already moved into the house. You would agree with that, wouldn't you?"

"Well, yes," she grudgingly compromised.

"Why don't you bring her over first thing in the morning, and we'll see how things go from there?"

"You're probably right. I realize adding another person to a household can change the whole complexion of things and I'm asking a lot of you two. But I don't think you'll be sorry. She's a lovely girl," Edith said.

"We're sure that she is," Georgette answered as she gave Maura a smile.

"I suppose I should get home and discuss this with Charles and Marie. I haven't said a word to them yet, and I'm about to burst a seam holding it in," she said with a giggle.

The other two women laughed at her last remark. Edith was such a sweet and generous person, but truth was truth: she would probably explode if she didn't tell them soon.

"Please keep in mind that Marie may not be interested in this plan," Maura warned. "Working in a restaurant may be the last thing that she wants to do with her life."

"Oh, don't be silly, Maura. She'll be delighted," Edith said, waving a hand to dismiss such a notion and pulling her blue woolen cloak around her shoulders. "Marie and I will be here early tomorrow morning," she continued while walking down the front steps.

"Not too early!" Georgette called after her as she smiled at the bustling figure now rushing toward home.

"We've had quite a day, and it's not even dinner time. I don't think I can take much more excitement," Georgette said.

"Oh, my goodness. Dinner!" Maura exclaimed, jumping from her chair.

"You needn't get too excited. It's just the two of us, and I'm in no big hurry to eat. Besides, we can have something simple," Georgette said.

"In all this commotion, I forgot to tell you that I'd invited Luther to dinner this evening. When I took his breakfast this morning, we agreed to meet after supper to further discuss some of our problems. And when he suggested that we meet after dinner, I told him to join us and we could talk after that," she explained.

"Well, I'm sure that he's not expecting a feast, especially after all the work we performed yesterday. Why is he being so pushy? Can't this wait? I'll walk down to the store and tell him that we've had some unexpected business today so you're too busy to entertain this evening," Georgette offered.

"No—I want to talk to Luther," Maura stated emphatically. "It's merely a matter of deciding upon something to fix for dinner."

"I see," Georgette said, pouting. "He's already got you playing to his tune."

"Now what is that supposed to mean? You've encouraged me to try and resolve our problems, but now that we're making progress, you're acting like a spoiled child."

"You're right. I have no business interfering. It's just my fear of losing you—of being alone—that makes me so quarrelsome. Forgive me, Maura. You know I want you and Luther to be happy. If you'll let me help you, I'm certain we can have something prepared for dinner by the time he arrives," she offered.

❧

Luther seemed to genuinely enjoy the company of the two women throughout dinner and even asked if Becca would soon be awakening so that he could see her.

"Why don't you two go into the parlor and visit? I'll clean up the kitchen," Georgette suggested when they had each finished a second cup of coffee. "I'll bring in dessert when I'm through," she continued since neither of them moved.

"We had planned to go to my place and visit. That way we won't be interfering with you and Becca," Luther explained.

"Besides, Edith may stop over—you know how impulsive she can be," Maura hastened to add, noting Georgette's wounded expression.

"Oh, of course. How silly of me! You two go along. I'm sure that you'd like to have some privacy," she replied in an attempt to sound cheerful.

Luther rose and retrieved his gray blanket-lined jacket from one of the pegs by the kitchen door.

"I think you'll need something heavier than your shawl this

evening," Luther said, encouraging Maura to move from the table.

"What? Oh, yes, I'll get my wool cape," she told him, taking his cue.

Meanwhile, Georgette continued working in the kitchen, saying nothing further as the couple prepared to leave.

"I think she's upset," Maura whispered as Luther held her cape.

"She'll be fine," he whispered back optimistically.

"We're leaving, Georgette. Come lock up behind us, please," Maura called from the hallway.

"My hands are wet. You go ahead and I'll lock it in just a minute," she called back to them.

Luther leaned forward to open the door as Maura gave him a faltering look. As if realizing that Maura would not leave until the door was locked behind them, Georgette appeared in the hallway, drying her hands on the blue calico apron tied around her waist. Georgette's red eyes belied the cheerful countenance she attempted to present, and had Luther not steered her out the door, Maura would have insisted that they remain.

"I don't like seeing her upset," Maura confided as they walked down the front steps.

"I know you don't. Upsetting Georgette is not what this is about, though. It's about our marriage," he replied.

"You're right, but it's still difficult," she said, feeling a quiver of pleasure as he placed his arm around her while they walked toward his house.

"Let me take your coat," he offered as they entered the parlor of his familiar house. "Why don't you sit over there on the sofa?" he proposed.

Maura carefully positioned herself at one end of the carved oak sofa, which had been upholstered in a cotton tapestry fabric in warm shades of brown and tan. He was soon back and sat down beside her, sitting so close that she found herself pinned between the arm of the sofa and Luther's body.

"I was so anxious for us to resume our conversation, I could hardly wait for dinner time to arrive," he told her, leaning down and placing a light kiss upon her lips.

"Did I tell you that Edith came looking for me when I was bringing your breakfast?" she asked, afraid that his continued kisses would prevent her from thinking coherently.

"Oh? And what was our good pastor's wife doing out and about so early this morning?" he asked.

"It seems that Marie McTavish, one of the dance hall girls who attended the Christmas dinner, went and talked to Charles last night. She wanted to know more about Jesus, and after he explained the plan of salvation, she accepted the Lord," Maura explained.

"Well, then, I'd say that the Christmas dinner was a successful ministry. I can just imagine Edith bustling about to spread the good news," he said, giving her a broad smile.

"That wasn't the only reason she came visiting. She was thrilled about Marie, of course, but she was also interested in finding suitable living accommodations for the new convert," she explained.

"And the perfect solution is with Georgette," he excitedly exclaimed.

"With Georgette and me," she corrected. "Edith's idea was that Marie come and live with us and help in the restaurant."

"But, Maura, don't you see? This must be God's answer to our problem. Marie needs a place to live, and Georgette needs someone to live with her, which frees you to return home. This is wonderful news," he said, pulling her into his arms with a tight embrace.

"Not so fast, Luther," she cautioned. "I can't just move out and leave Georgette living with a complete stranger."

"Why not? You two were strangers," he rebutted.

"Not really. We had developed a friendship while on

board the ship and during the time we lived here with you. There was no question that we could compatibly live under the same roof, and we had a vested interest in making the situation work in order to support ourselves," she reminded him.

"She and this Marie can become friends, and they'll both realize the fact that they need to get along. After all, nothing is going to change their need to support themselves. At least not right away," he again rebutted. "When is Marie moving in?" he asked, his voice filled with excitement.

"Well, we haven't agreed that she can—at least not yet. We—"

"Why not? It's a perfect solution for all of us," he interupted.

"We want to see if we're compatible first. Marie is coming to meet us tomorrow. If the meeting goes well, she will come to work for us during the days and return to the Wilsons at night. Then—and only then—will we suggest that she move in with us. We did agree to begin furnishing an additional upstairs bedroom for her," Maura explained.

"Wait a minute! What's all this talk about we? Georgette's the only one who has to get along with her, and I'm sure that she'll make more effort if she knows you've decided to return home. The two of them should be deciding how they want to operate the restaurant and if they want to begin furnishing additional rooms. It will only complicate matters if they begin to rely on you—Georgette already does too much of that. Besides, Marie can have your room. It's the answer to my prayers," he solemnly told her.

"It may be the answer to my prayers also, Luther. But I think we're going to need time to make sure. We have several differing ideas that we need to resolve—"

"You could move back tomorrow," he interrupted, ignoring her protests. "I can bring the wagon over first thing in the morning, and I'm sure that Michael and Charles will be glad to help. You can run the store while we're doing that."

He gave her a reassuring hug with a look of complete satisfaction written on his face.

"No!"

"No? What do you mean, no?" he asked, turning sideways on the sofa to look at her.

"I want to take the time to effect a lasting reconciliation; I've told you that. Luther, I don't plan to give up my interest in the restaurant. The money we used to purchase that home was an unexpected inheritance from Rachel Windsor. It was her dream to open a restaurant and boarding house in California. Georgette and I are fulfilling that dream not only for ourselves but also in memory of Rachel. That may be hard for you to understand, but I'd like to think that we are being good stewards and providing a much-needed service to this community, as well as supporting ourselves," she explained carefully.

"You don't need to support yourself any longer. That's my job, and I want to do it. Let Georgette and Marie fulfill the dream. It doesn't have to be you. Besides, you won't have time for working at the restaurant," he stated and then pulled her close, attempting to capture her lips.

Quickly she turned her head. "No, Luther. We won't solve our problems by everything being exactly as you say and then your quieting me with a kiss. My resentment would begin to rise, and eventually your kisses would become bitter. I don't want that to happen," she replied.

"What is the answer, then? We do everything as you say so that you'll be happy?" he asked in an irritated voice.

"No. If we did that, you wouldn't be happy. After a while, you probably would cease to want even my kisses," she replied, smiling weakly. "I don't want that to happen, either."

"So? What do we do?"

She looked thoughtful. "Would you object if I planned the menus and ordered the supplies for the restaurant?" she ventured.

"Well, no. That would probably work. Perhaps you could

arrange to go over menus with Georgette and help at the restaurant two or three mornings a week," he answered.

She gave him an endearing smile in return. "I would like a kiss," she stated.

He laughed heartily and promptly accommodated her request.

"Now, for the next matter," she said, moving from his fervent hold. "We need to come to an agreement about when I will move back home. I know you want it to be tomorrow. However, I think three months would give us enough time to be sure that Georgette is comfortable with the new arrangement," she said sweetly.

"Absolutely not!" he bellowed. "I'll not wait three months—one month is the absolute maximum I'll agree to!"

"Six weeks?" she questioned.

"The first day of February. You will sleep under this roof commencing the first day of February and not a day past. Do I have your word?"

His folded arms and furrowed brow gave evidence that he would brook no further argument.

"You have my word. Shall we seal it with a kiss?" she inquired, moving toward him.

"If anyone had ever told me that you would totally capture my heart and mind, I would have laughed. Just look at me—a complete fool over the woman I felt obligated to marry. Do you know how much I love you?" he asked, pulling her toward him.

Before she could answer, his lips were upon hers with an urgency and obvious desire that soon inflamed her whole being. Returning his passion, she surrendered her lips and returned his kiss with mounting ardor. His hand cupped the nape of her neck, which pulled her even closer and held her captive to the intensity of his yearning.

"We must stop this," Maura murmured, reluctantly pushing away from him.

"Why? We are married," he argued, attempting to pull her back into his arms.

"But I don't feel married, Luther," she answered.

"I'd like to change that! It's you who's not willing," he replied. The sorrow in his eyes was apparent.

"I'm willing, Luther. But I believe that it would be better to wait until I've moved back home and we are truly living together. A new beginning to our marriage, with both of us eager and willing to share our lives. Does that make sense to you?"

He waited for what seemed an eternity and then turned toward her with a smile emerging upon his face.

"Why don't we really start over? Let's have a church wedding, like you dreamed of, with our friends there with us. I'm sure that Charles would be pleased to perform the ceremony, and it would give Edith another project to oversee. What do you think?" he asked, his excitement now contagious.

"And we could have a small reception at the restaurant," she added. "Oh, Luther, it would be grand. Thank you for being so thoughtful," she said, spontaneously giving him a hug.

"Let's go tell Georgette," he suggested, rising from the sofa and offering her his hand.

"I probably should get back, but I'd rather wait to tell Georgette. I think she'll accept it more once she's gotten acquainted with Marie."

"You're probably right. Just remember this: you agreed to move back by the first of February at the latest," he reminded her.

"What do you think of January twenty-ninth as our wedding day?" she asked.

"It sounds fine. Is there something significant about that particular day?" he inquired.

"Yes. It's my parents' wedding anniversary, and they've been married almost forty years. Perhaps it will be a good date for us, also," she said, giving him a smile.

"Then January twenty-ninth it is," he replied while retrieving her cape from the small closet in the hallway.

## thirteen

Marie McTavish invaded the lives of Maura, Georgette, and Becca with an enthusiasm and joy that nobody could ignore. The gifts of her newfound salvation and friends were a seemingly constant source of delight to her, and she expressed it in every way possible. Having left seven brothers in Ohio, she was immediately captivated by Becca's many charms. In fact, it seemed as if the baby were always riding on her hip.

"You're spoiling her," Georgette mildly scolded as Marie walked into the kitchen early one morning with Becca in her usual position, resting on Marie's hip.

"Love doesn't spoil children. It makes them blossom—just like flowers. Untended flowers soon wither and die; untended children do the same. Maybe not a physical death, but in other ways that damage and scar them for life. I won't indulge her whenever the time comes that she needs correction, but she hasn't reached that time in her life just yet," Marie answered, with a wisdom beyond her years.

"I've never seen you so serious, Marie. I'm sorry if I upset you," Georgette responded, observing the pained look on her new friend's face.

"It's all right. Guess I'm just thinking about my own childhood," Marie replied while measuring out ingredients for a batch of buttermilk biscuits.

"Tell me about it," Georgette urged.

"Nothing much to tell. Too many kids, too little money. I watched my ma turn into an old woman by the time she was thirty. She died shortly after my youngest brother turned two. I was the oldest child and the only daughter. Guess that says it all. I had to give up going to school when Ma died. All my time was taken up cooking, sewing, doing farm chores, and tending my brothers. When I turned sixteen, I told Pa he'd better find someone else to take over. He didn't take too kindly to the idea, but I stuck to my guns. I figured he'd never look for a wife as long as he had me around, and I sure didn't plan to die like Mama. Soon he found him a widow lady to marry. The day she moved in, I moved out."

"Where did you go?" Georgette asked, fascinated by the unfolding story. Although her own family was not considered wealthy, they had never wanted for anything.

"I hate to admit it, but I took the egg money and used it to pay for my passage to St. Louis. However, without any education or experience, I found that there weren't many jobs available. So I went to work cooking in a restaurant. One day the owner of a saloon down the street asked if I wanted a job making twice as much money. Unfortunately, I jumped at the chance," she answered, shaking her head in obvious disgust at what she had done.

"You were young and made a mistake; we all do. What's important is that we learn from those mistakes," Georgette consoled.

"I'm afraid I was a long time learning! I saved enough money to get myself to California, hoping to get a fresh start. Trouble is, I used up all my money getting here. I told myself I'd work in a saloon only for a little while, just long enough to get some money together and figure out what I wanted to do."

"What city were you living in?" Georgette asked, taking the baby while Marie rolled out the biscuits.

"Here. In Placerville. Jake Grisby, the owner of the saloon, was in San Francisco the day I arrived. He goes there whenever he needs to hire new girls," she explained.

"Why?" Georgette asked.

"To watch for new female arrivals. He has quite a line—but let's not go into that. Anyway, I came to Placerville and ended up worse than when I'd been in St. Louis. Jake always found a reason not to pay us. He figured if we ever got ahold of any money, we'd take off—and he was right about that. You can't just walk to another town from Placerville—at least not one where you could make a living."

"I'll bet you've had lots of men asking for your hand. Women are scarce around here. Why didn't you accept one and get out of that place if it was so bad?" Georgette asked.

"Oh, sure. I had marriage proposals. But most of the men that came in the saloon couldn't support a wife. Besides, what little gold they found was used to buy liquor and more supplies because they were determined they'd strike the mother lode the next time they went out in the hills. And the few men of means that came around weren't about to marry a saloon girl. Believe me, there wasn't an easy answer. At least not until I listened to Pastor Wilson," she explained.

"I'm so glad that you came to our Christmas dinner. Just think, if Jake hadn't closed the saloon Christmas day, you'd most likely still be working for him. I'll bet he's been seething ever since," Georgette said, giggling.

"I think you're probably right. I'm hoping I can save up enough money to help a couple of the other girls get out of there someday. Working there is a poor excuse for a life," Marie explained while she wiped the flour from her hands.

❧

"Well, what are you two so serious about?" Maura asked as she entered the back door, which allowed a gust of cold air into the room.

"It's getting colder, isn't it?" Georgette asked while Maura hung her coat on one of the pegs by the back door.

"Yes," Maura answered, moving toward the fireplace to warm her hands.

"What took you out so early this morning?" Marie inquired, giving Maura a sweet smile.

"Luther and I wanted to meet with Pastor Wilson to go over

our wedding plans. You know how Luther is—he didn't want to leave everything until the last minute," Maura explained.

"My goodness, Maura, you've got almost three weeks. How much can there be to discuss?" Georgette asked in a voice filled with irritation.

Although Georgette had been attempting to act supportive of their reconciliation and impending wedding, it was obvious that she hadn't totally adjusted to the thought of Maura's moving back with Luther.

"Luther just wants everything to go smoothly," Maura replied.

"He just wants to be sure that you don't back out," Georgette rebutted.

"Back out? Georgette, I'm already married to Luther. This wedding is more for me than Luther. He wanted me to have the kind of wedding I've always dreamed about. One I could remember with fondness," Maura answered, hurt at Georgette's attitude.

"Right now, Luther Buchanan would do anything to get you back to that store. He's probably already figuring how much more money he's going to make having you there working all the time," she retorted, her facial expressions forming a giant pout.

Maura couldn't refrain from breaking into laughter at Georgette's dramatic exhibition.

"Just what are you laughing about?" Georgette demanded.

"You!" Maura replied. "I'm surprised that you're not stomping your feet. Honestly, Georgette, you're acting more childish than a two-year-old."

"Is that right? Well, perhaps if you were in my position, you'd be stomping your feet, too! I'm about to lose my best friend, and it's not a very pleasant feeling," Georgette replied.

"Lose your best friend? You're not losing me, Georgette. I'm only moving down the street," Maura responded. "I think we need to have a talk. Let's go in the parlor. Marie, would you mind looking after Becca?" she asked while ushering Georgette toward the other room.

"Sit down," Maura instructed.

Georgette plopped down into the wooden rocking chair and furiously rocked back and forth.

"You know, Georgette, I remember a young girl I met on a ship sailing to California. She became my friend, and I thought she wanted only the best for me. It appears that what she really wanted was what was best for me—as long as it was what was best for her also."

"That's not true," Georgette fired back, jumping up from the chair. "I still want what is best for you, but I'm not convinced that going to live with Luther is what's best."

"Georgette, it's not been so long ago that you were seeing the kinder, more gentle side of Luther. But now that we've made progress in reconciling our differences, you've changed your mind. Your attitude makes me think that you're more concerned about losing my help in the restaurant than anything else."

"I'm hurt that you could even think such a thing," Georgette responded, tears forming in her eyes. "I suppose the real truth is that I've come to rely upon you, Maura. If—I mean, when— you leave, it's going to be like leaving my family all over again. I'll be alone," she said, her voice now soft and pitiful.

"Georgette, Luther has agreed that I can continue to help here at the restaurant. And I plan to do just that. Besides, you must remember that you have Becca and Marie. Marie is such a dear, and the two of you are already getting along famously. I truly believe that the Lord has sent her to us for this very reason."

"The Lord knows my heart, and He knows it's you I want here," Georgette answered, still unwilling to concede.

"The Lord knows what we need, and He provides. Nowhere in the Bible does it say that He provides what we want.

Remember that, Georgette. It's a difficult lesson—one that most of us don't fully master in a lifetime."

"I'll try to be happy for you, Maura, but I want you to remember that if things turn sour again, you've always got a home here."

"Thank you, Georgette," she said, giving the girl a hug.

"I must admit that I'm surprised that Luther has agreed you can continue to help with our business," Georgette said.

"I think he realizes how important the restaurant has become to me, and he also knows how much I'll miss being with you and Becca. He truly has changed, Georgette. In fact, now I don't doubt his love for me. We've both had changes of heart, and I think we're going to begin our marriage for all the right reasons when we have our wedding in a few weeks."

"I hope so, Maura. The last thing I want is for you to be hurt again," Georgette responded, obviously unconvinced that Luther's motives were genuine.

❧

During the next week the weather turned colder, and on several mornings the Placerville inhabitants had awakened to a light dusting of snow. This morning, however, it had continued. Maura glanced out the window, watching as the large, wet flakes began to accumulate, the tree branches already laden with the additional weight.

"Why the worried look?" Marie asked as she walked into the kitchen and poured a large mug of coffee.

"Luther left for San Francisco yesterday. I tried to convince him to wait until the weather cleared, but he said that would mean holding off until spring," Maura replied, pushing the cream pitcher across the table toward Marie.

"He'll be fine. I'm sure that he's been making the trip for quite a few years now and knows how to take care of himself. Quit your worrying! It'll do him no good, and it certainly won't do you any good," Marie advised.

"You're right, but it's easier said than done."

Marie smiled and placed an arm around her new friend. "If the three of us commit to keep him in our prayers until his safe return, perhaps it will be easier for you."

"Thank you, Marie. It would mean a great deal to know that you and Georgette are praying for Luther's safety. I'll be doing the same," she answered. "By the way, have I told you how pleased I am that God sent you to us?"

"Well, not exactly. However, Georgette has told me that I'm God's answer to Luther's prayers," she responded, with a broad smile.

Maura chuckled at the remark. "I think you are God's answer to many prayers. But, in addition to that, I am very pleased to be counted among your friends and am happy that you've come to live here."

"Thank you, Maura. I'll be forever in your debt—and Georgette's," Marie solemnly stated.

"You're not in my debt, Marie. You've more than earned your keep around here. Without your help, it would have been several more weeks before we could open the restaurant. And now look at us—we've been in full operation for almost two weeks."

"Speaking of which, I'd better get busy. We'll have customers expecting breakfast soon," Marie answered, just as the front door slammed shut.

"Georgette! Where have you been? I didn't even realize that you'd left the house," Maura inquired, her concern evident.

Georgette knocked the snow from her boots and then moved toward the kitchen stove to warm herself. "I wanted to remove some of the snow from the front steps before our customers begin arriving," she explained. "It's really coming down, so my efforts will probably be in vain," she continued while doffing her heavy wool coat and gloves.

"We may not have many customers if it's that bad out there," Maura commented.

"Don't count on that," Marie countered. "The men around

here have become used to a hearty home-cooked breakfast. Believe me, they'll be here. I'd better get out back and bring in some more wood," she said, reaching for her heavy coat hanging by the kitchen door.

"Michael tells me that it looks as if this promises to be the worst storm in several years," Georgette commented as she rubbed her hands together in front of the fire. "He said anyone caught out in this weather would be fortunate to survive."

Maura felt her heart sink in her chest. "Michael thinks it's going to be that bad?" she inquired, attempting to hide her growing concern.

"He said it looks like we're in for a good one and there's no telling when it might stop. A couple of the old-timers that have been around these parts for years told him from the look of the skies, we'll probably be snowed in for quite a while. I hope Luther's got his supplies well stocked," she commented.

"Luther's gone," Maura quietly answered.

"Gone? Gone where?" Georgette asked with surprise.

"San Francisco."

"San Francisco? Why on earth did he leave this time of year—with so little time before your wedding? Did he have supplies coming in?" she inquired.

"He didn't tell me much. I asked him to wait, but he said he had to go. I know it wasn't for supplies because he didn't take the wagons. He was going alone on his horse and said he should be back in plenty of time for the wedding."

"Isn't that just like him? That man is so selfish—always thinking of himself and causing—"

"Georgette, I really don't want to hear your unkind remarks. I'm concerned about Luther, and what would help me is to know that my friends are praying for his safe return rather than criticizing his mysterious actions," Maura said as Marie bustled in the back door with an armful of wood, her hair turned temporarily white from the trip outdoors.

The breakfast crowd began arriving, and the morning

passed quickly. It was shortly after ten o'clock when Maura noticed Georgette as she sat talking with Michael, who had returned for coffee and a break from his work. This arrangement had become a recent habit, and Maura was pleased that the two of them seemed to be forming a caring relationship.

"Where are you going?" Georgette called out just as Maura reached the front door.

"I promised Luther that I'd take care of the store during the afternoon while he's gone. I'll be back to help with supper, and things are well underway for the noon crowd. So I don't think you'll need me. If you do, send word to Charles, and I'm sure he'll relieve me at the store so that I can return," she replied as she tied on her heavy wool bonnet.

"Wait, Maura. I'll go with you. It's treacherous walking out there, and we sure don't want you falling down," Michael offered.

"No, no. I don't want to take you away. I can make it just fine," she replied.

"I'll hear nothing of the kind," he sternly admonished as he rose from the chair.

Once they were out the door, she was glad to have Michael's assistance. The snow made walking nearly impossible, and the high winds made it difficult to see so much as a hand in front of one's face.

"It's a real white-out," Michael shouted as they pushed against the wind.

Maura didn't attempt to reply. It was taking every ounce of strength she had just to remain upright for the short distance. In fact, it would have been impossible without Michael's help. Once inside the store, she removed the "Closed" sign from the door and carefully lit several of the oil lamps.

"I'll get a fire going for you before I leave," Michael offered, and Maura didn't resist. "By the way, Georgette didn't seem to know why Luther had ventured off to San Francisco in the middle of winter. Did he confide in you before leaving town?"

he inquired while keeping his attention on the wood he was stacking in the fireplace.

She was chilled to the bone, and although she knew she could muster the strength to get the fire started, it would take her much longer than it would take Michael. Watching as he adeptly laid the wood in place and set a match to the tinder, she smiled as the fire began to lick upward toward the larger logs and then answered, "I really don't know, Michael. He said he had some business that had to be taken care of and he'd be back in time for the wedding."

She hoped he would say something to bolster her spirits and help assuage the growing fear in the pit of her stomach.

"It ought to warm up in here pretty soon. Why don't you sit close by and dry off," he suggested after a brief pause. "Looks like I'd better bring in some more wood before I go so it'll be good and dry before it's needed," he said, surveying the sparse pile by the stone hearth.

"Thank you, Michael. I appreciate your help," she said, sitting down in the chair he'd pulled close to the fireplace.

"I'm glad to help, Maura. I just wish that Luther wouldn't have taken off in this kind of weather. He knows better."

"It wasn't snowing when he left," she said in his defense.

"No, but he knows enough about this country to realize there was a possibility of something like this." Seeing the pained look on her face, he quickly added, "Luther knows how to take care of himself. I'm just glad he's traveling on horseback instead of with wagons. He stands more of a chance of getting through without wagons. Besides, he's made more trips to San Francisco than anyone else around Placerville. If anyone can find his way through this storm, it'll be Luther. Guess I'd better get back to work," he continued while walking toward the front door.

"Thanks again, Michael."

"I'll come back around four o'clock and fetch you," he told her and quickly exited. A rush of cold air and a light layer of snow entered the store as Michael left.

*Doubt there will be much business here today,* she thought as she began walking about the store and deciding what tasks would keep her busy during the next several hours.

Placing a pot of coffee over the fire, she was heartened when two old miners came wandering in to sit by the hearth and play a game of checkers. They were familiar faces, men who now spent more time in town than they did mining. Maura had learned that when their funds ran low, they'd go back into the hills until they'd accumulated enough gold dust to keep them going a while longer.

They drank steaming coffee from large tin mugs and talked with each other, commenting from time to time on the weather and shaking their heads in obvious disgust.

"Luther say when he'd be back?" one of them asked as they were preparing to leave the store.

"He didn't say exactly," she replied honestly.

"Did he take the wagons?" the other inquired.

"No, he didn't go for supplies," she answered.

"How 'bout I go out there and take care of the animals for ya? Was he planning on you doing that, or did he make other arrangements?"

"I'm not sure," she replied, having given no thought to the horses that probably should have been tended earlier in the day.

"Don't you worry, missus. We'll take care of 'em while he's gone. Luther's done plenty for us in the past, so it's the least we can do."

"I sure do thank you," Maura answered.

"Thank you, Lord, for once again providing me with assistance," she whispered as the men left the store.

Michael reappeared shortly after four o'clock and escorted her back to the house. The savory aroma of beef stew and cornbread, together with the warmth from the kitchen, greeted them as they opened the back door.

"Why'd you come clear around back?" Marie inquired as the couple entered.

"I convinced Michael to come around here so that we wouldn't track all this mess into the front," Maura replied, attempting to stomp the snow from her shoes while shaking her skirt.

"You shouldn't have been concerned about that," Georgette told them as she entered the kitchen. "I've spent a good part of the day wiping up the mess created by this snowstorm."

"Well, I hope that we've saved you a little work," Maura said, giving her friend a hug.

"I'm glad you're back here. If this snow keeps up, I'm not going to hear of you going back to that store tomorrow," Georgette warned. "Michael agrees with me, don't you, Michael?" she asked.

"Well, I don't think it would be wise," he cautiously agreed.

"Let's wait until tomorrow before we make any decisions," Maura suggested. "What needs to be done toward finishing dinner?" she asked, intentionally changing the subject.

"Everything's ready, but I'm not expecting much of a crowd tonight," Marie said. "I didn't prepare near as much as we normally do. Hope I didn't misjudge folks."

"We'll find something to serve them if we run out of stew, Marie. Folks are more likely to come and eat when they have to be out and about early in the day. Once they get home, they're probably going to stay put," Maura agreed.

The next morning the snow had stopped, but the winds continued gusting, causing large drifts to form in their wake. Maura peeked out the parlor window and was greeted by dazzling snowdrifts along the front of the house that completely covered the lower half of the windows.

*We're really snowed in,* she thought, sure that they couldn't possibly open the front door without being prepared to tunnel through the five-foot-high drifts. Marie walked into the parlor and positioned herself alongside Maura.

"Guess we won't have to cook for anybody except ourselves today, will we?" Marie asked, giving Maura a pensive look.

"He's going to be just fine," she reassured Maura. "I just feel it in my soul."

"Thank you, Marie," Maura said, giving her a hug. "I think I'd like a cup of coffee," she said, deliberately changing the subject. She didn't want to think about where Luther might be. If she did, she was afraid where those thoughts might lead her.

During the weeks that followed, the snow and winds finally abated. Through the combined efforts of the townspeople, they had finally dug themselves out. Although the weather remained frigid and the sun couldn't seem to emit enough heat to melt the snow, life returned to a semblance of normality. But still no word was received from Luther, and the few new folks who came to town had seen or heard nothing of the man whom Maura doggedly described to them.

❧

"I don't know what you can be thinking, Maura. You're only going to cause yourself further distress and heartache. Please tell me that you'll cease this nonsense immediately," Georgette chided her friend.

"You'd just as well stop badgering me, Georgette. I've made up my mind," Maura asserted staunchly.

"This is utter foolishness!"

"You need not take part if that's the way you feel. Just stay here and carry out your chores as usual. I'll not hold it against you," Maura said as she placed an iron kettle filled with water over the fire to heat.

"Do you really believe that he's going to magically appear just because it's January twenty-ninth?" Georgette asked impatiently.

"We set January twenty-ninth as our wedding day and I'm going to be there—on time—for the wedding," Maura replied stubbornly.

Maura noted the look exchanged by Marie and Georgette, although she was sure that it wasn't intended for her eyes.

*They think I'm crazy,* she thought, *but I know this is what I'm supposed to do.*

Against Georgette's wishes, a notice had been placed on the front door of the restaurant for the last three days stating that they would be closed for business today. The two of them had argued about the circumstances: Georgette did not want her friend to be disappointed or embarrassed when Luther failed to appear, whereas Maura was sure that the wedding would turn out as planned. Only Marie remained silent.

Once the water was heated, Marie assisted Maura in filling the tub and then left her to enjoy a warm bath, the soothing fragrance of lavender oil filling the room.

"Why don't you try and talk some sense into her," Georgette whispered to Marie as Georgette exited the kitchen and entered the hallway.

"No, I don't think it would be proper for me to become involved in this. Besides, Georgette, Maura is a grown woman. I'm sure she understands that Luther probably won't be at the church. However, if she feels this strongly about keeping her commitment to the wedding plans, why are you so determined to stop her?"

"It's just silly. After all, they're already married. Why should she put herself through this added pain?"

"I'm not sure why she's so stubborn, but I'll certainly not be the one attempting to stop her," Marie said firmly. "I've got to get upstairs. I told Maura I'd help her get dressed. Are you going to get ready or not? She's planning on you being her attendant."

"Oh, there won't be any wedding. But if she's going to get ready, I guess I will, too. Have you seen Michael this morning?" Georgette inquired.

"No. Isn't he supposed to stand with Luther?" she asked.

"Yes," Georgette replied, shaking her head. "I wonder if he's going to go to the trouble of getting ready or if he has more sense than the rest of us," she mused, following Marie up the stairway.

Maura allowed the warm water to envelop her as she slid into its depths, pushing all thoughts from her mind as she soaked in the sweet-smelling fragrance. When the water finally turned cool, she stepped out of the tub and dried herself in front of the fire. Wrapping herself in the warm quilt that Marie had left for her, she made her way upstairs to her bedroom.

"I don't think I've ever seen such a beautiful wedding dress," Marie said as Maura walked in the room.

"Thank you, Marie. I'm quite fond of it myself and feel quite fortunate. How many brides are able to wear their wedding dresses more than once?"

"Not many, I'm sure," Marie answered.

"I'll be fine, Marie," Maura confided. "Even if Luther doesn't make it, I'll be fine," she affirmed, realizing that both of her friends were worried how she would react if Luther didn't appear.

"Georgette cares about you very much, Maura. At first I thought she was jealous you were leaving, but now I think she's truly concerned that you'll be deeply wounded if the wedding doesn't take place," Marie confided.

"I know she means well, Marie. Georgette is a dear girl whose friendship I treasure, but she must realize that I'm keeping things in proper order—God first, Luther second, and then others. I must at least try to honor my word to my husband. I hope that she'll understand my reasons, and you need not worry—I'm not angry with her. How could I be? I know she's merely trying to protect me," Maura said as she stepped into the silk wedding gown.

"You look lovely," Georgette complimented her friend as she walked into the room and once again beheld the ivory silk wedding dress. "I had forgotten just how beautiful your dress is," she continued, softly touching the long sleeves, which were accented with the same ivory lace that surrounded the bertha.

"You're quite a sight yourself," Maura said, admiring the deep green silk gown that the two of them had sewn especially for this occasion. "That color is lovely with your hair and skin. You should wear it often."

"Thank you, Maura," Georgette said, giving her friend a broad smile.

"Let me get your shoes," Marie offered, retrieving from the closet the low-heeled ivory shoes decorated with tiny lace bows.

"Would you like me to fashion your hair in finger curls like last time?" Georgette asked, picking up Maura's hairbrush.

"I'd like that very much," Maura replied, giving her friend a kiss on the cheek.

After several attempts, Georgette and Marie finally agreed that the bride's hair passed inspection. Carefully, Georgette placed the coronet headpiece of crystal-beaded flowers and waxed orange blossoms that held the lace veil on Maura's head.

"She has no bouquet to carry," Marie commented forlornly to Georgette.

"Of course she does. Wait until you see it. Maura's mother made it, and it matches her headpiece. It's absolutely stunning," Georgette confided as if Maura weren't even present.

"Where is your bouquet?" Georgette asked looking about the room.

"In the second drawer of the chiffonier," Maura answered, watching as Georgette pulled the small bouquet fashioned from ribbons, lace, and waxed orange blossoms and leaves from the depths of the bureau.

"Oh, Maura, it's lovely," Marie agreed, admiring the delicate arrangement.

"Thank you, and thank you both for your help. I think we're ready, with time to spare," she added.

"I just hope that Michael gets here with the buggy," Georgette said just as a knock sounded at the front door. Waffles bounded from the room and raced down the steps, his instinctive barking at any intrusion now expected by the residents of the household.

Georgette followed the dog downstairs and found herself hoping that Luther would be standing there to greet her. Instead, it was Michael, dressed in his best dark blue suit, and the buggy was parked in front of the house.

"Is she ready?" Michael whispered.

"Yes, but believe me, I tried my best all morning to dissuade her. She wouldn't hear of it," Georgette divulged.

"I haven't seen anything of Luther, and I think if he were in town the store would be open or there'd be some sign of him. I stopped by the Wilsons' place earlier today, but they hadn't heard from him, either. However, Charles and Edith said they'd be at the church as planned. I'm afraid everyone's going to be there except Luther. I hope this isn't going to turn into a disaster for Maura," he said in a compassionate voice.

"Hello, Michael," Maura called out from the top of the stairs. "Thank you for being so prompt."

"My! Don't you look lovely," Michael complimented. "How fortunate can a man be? Escorting such lovely ladies doesn't happen very often. This is truly a pleasure. Let me help you with your wraps," he offered.

"I'll go and get Becca," Marie offered while the others were retrieving their coats.

All of them smiled when Marie returned with the baby. Marie had gathered the baby's downy fuzz together and placed a tiny bow on her head.

"She's dressed for the occasion, also," Marie said, giggling at Becca as she handed the infant over to Georgette and allowed Michael to assist her into her own coat.

The brief ride to the church seemed even shorter today. Maura strained to catch sight of Luther or glimpse any evidence that he might be present at the church. But she didn't see any sign of his horse or the buggy that he used on Sundays and special occasions. From the number of carriages tied outside the church, it appeared many of the folks from town had braved the cold.

"Looks like you're going to have quite a few folks celebrating with you," Michael ventured as they pulled to a stop at the back of the church.

Maura merely nodded her head and allowed him to assist her down from the buggy.

"I'll take you in and come back for Marie and Georgette," he instructed. "That way you'll have time to talk to Charles before it's time to begin." He escorted her into the back of the church and toward the small room where she was to meet the pastor.

The tinkling sounds of the piano lingered in the air as she entered the room. Pastor Wilson was there—alone—sitting in one of the chairs and reading his Bible.

"Maura, don't you look lovely. What a beautiful bride you are," he complimented warmly, rising from the overstuffed chair and placing his Bible on the small oak table sitting between two of the chairs.

"Thank you, Charles. Have you seen anything of Luther yet?" she inquired, her voice filled with expectancy.

"I'm afraid not, my dear," he replied. "But there's still time. The service isn't due to begin for another fifteen minutes, and I'm not opposed to waiting a bit longer than that if need be."

"Luther believes in punctuality. If he's not here at the appointed time, he'll not be coming," she stated.

"Now, now, my dear. Occasionally life can cause delays. We can't always adhere to the ticking of a clock. Why don't you sit down, and we'll read some scripture and pray a bit," he offered.

Maura carefully backed toward the chair, the whalebone stays causing her no small amount of difficulty in maneuvering. She smiled. "I think I'd rather stand, if you don't mind.

It took a great deal of time getting in and out of the buggy, and I don't think I'm up to the challenge quite so soon," she explained.

"Certainly. I understand," he said, leafing through the Bible for a passage that he hoped would lessen Maura's obvious concerns about Luther and his whereabouts. "Are you familiar with the words of Matthew 6:25, Maura?"

"Would that be a passage about worry and anxiety?" she inquired.

"Exactly," he said with a smile. "Would you like me to read it aloud?"

"Please," she replied, slowly beginning to relax.

Charles settled into the chair and quietly began to read. Maura listened carefully as he recited these words: "Behold the fowls of the air: for they sow not, neither do they reap, nor gather into barns; yet your heavenly Father feedeth them. Are ye not much better than they?"

Both Charles and Maura turned as a voice behind them continued, "Which of you by taking thought can add one cubit unto his stature?"

"Luther!" Maura exclaimed, rushing to his outstretched arms. "Oh, Luther, I was so worried. You should never have made that trip. Were you caught in the blizzard?"

He smiled down at her and reached into the embroidered blue satin waistcoat he had worn for their wedding in San Francisco. Pulling out his watch, he clicked it open. "I'm afraid we'll have to wait until after the wedding for explanations if we're going to begin on time," he told her.

"I told you he believed in punctuality," she said, looking over her shoulder toward Charles.

"There's time for just one thing before we go into the church," he said, reaching into the breast pocket of his coat and pulling out a black velvet box. "This is why I went to San Francisco," he revealed as he opened the case.

"Oh, Luther," she said, stunned at the beauty of his gift.

"Do you like it?" he inquired, his eyes twinkling at her obvious delight.

"How could anyone not like it?" she asked, staring at the most beautiful brooch she had ever seen. The circular silver pin was set with a hexagonal emerald surrounded by six sparkling diamonds.

"Turn it over," he instructed as she lifted it from the bed of ivory silk inside the container.

Carefully, she revolved the pin and saw the engraved words on the back. *Maura, you have changed my heart forever. I'll love you always. Luther.*

"Thank you," she said as her finger traced over the words. Turning the pin over, her finger caught on a tiny clasp and the pin snapped open, revealing a delicate watch.

"I thought you might like to have a watch to make sure that I'm punctual, since I'm always checking the time," he said, giving her a smile.

"Oh, Luther, what a wonderful gift," she said, once again looking down at the pin.

The preacher looked across her hand and eyed the gift. "It would appear that you'd better pin that on her gown, or we're going to be late in spite of those timepieces."

This wedding was everything that Maura had originally hoped for. Most important, their vows were exchanged in love with hope for their future together as husband and wife. When Pastor Wilson announced that Luther could kiss his bride, this time it took no prompting from Maura.

After Luther pulled her into his arms, his lips sought hers with a fervent desire that touched the depths of her soul. She leaned into him and returned the kiss with an intense longing. A longing to begin her life anew as his wife—her life as Maura Buchanan.

# *A Letter To Our Readers*

Dear Reader:

In order that we might better contribute to your reading enjoyment, we would appreciate your taking a few minutes to respond to the following questions. When completed, please return to the following:

Rebecca Germany, Managing Editor
Heartsong Presents
PO Box 719
Uhrichsville, Ohio 44683

1. Did you enjoy reading *Changes of the Heart?*
   ❑ Very much. I would like to see more books
      by this author!
   ❑ Moderately
      I would have enjoyed it more if _____

   _____

2. Are you a member of **Heartsong Presents**? ❑Yes ❑No
   If no, where did you purchase this book? _____

   _____

3. What influenced your decision to purchase this
   book? (Check those that apply.)

   ❑ Cover        ❑ Back cover copy

   ❑ Title        ❑ Friends

   ❑ Publicity    ❑ Other_____

4. How would you rate, on a scale from 1 (poor) to 5
   (superior), the cover design? _____

5. On a scale from 1 (poor) to 10 (superior), please rate the following elements.

    ___Heroine    ___Plot

    ___Hero    ___Inspirational theme

    ___Setting    ___Secondary characters

6. What settings would you like to see covered in **Heartsong Presents** books?_____

_____

_____

7. What are some inspirational themes you would like to see treated in future books?_____

_____

_____

8. Would you be interested in reading other **Heartsong Presents** titles?   ❏ Yes   ❏ No

9. Please check your age range:
   ❏ Under 18   ❏ 18-24   ❏ 25-34
   ❏ 35-45   ❏ 46-55   ❏ Over 55

10. How many hours per week do you read? _____

Name _____

Occupation _____

Address _____

City_____ State_____ Zip_____

# *Only You*

# ·········· Presents ··········

## Great Inspirational Romance at a Great Price!

**Heartsong Presents** books are inspirational romances in contemporary and historical settings, designed to give you an enjoyable, spirit-lifting reading experience. You can choose wonderfully written titles from some of today's best authors like Peggy Darty, Sally Laity, Tracie Peterson, Colleen L. Reece, Lauraine Snelling, and many others.

*When ordering quantities less than twelve, above titles are $2.95 each.*
*Not all titles may be available at time of order.*

---

SEND TO: Heartsong Presents Reader's Service
P.O. Box 719, Uhrichsville, Ohio 44683

Please send me the items checked above. I am enclosing $_____.
(please add $1.00 to cover postage per order. OH add 6.25% tax. NJ add 6%). Send check or money order, no cash or C.O.D.s, please.
**To place a credit card order, call 1-800-847-8270.**

NAME _____

ADDRESS _____

CITY/STATE _____ ZIP _____

HPS 11-98

# Heartsong Presents
# *Love Stories Are Rated G!*

That's for godly, gratifying, and of course, great! If you love a thrilling love story, but don't appreciate the sordidness of some popular paperback romances, **Heartsong Presents** is for you. In fact, **Heartsong Presents** is the *only inspirational romance book club*, the only one featuring love stories where Christian faith is the primary ingredient in a marriage relationship.

Sign up today to receive your first set of four, never before published Christian romances. Send no money now; you will receive a bill with the first shipment. You may cancel at any time without obligation, and if you aren't completely satisfied with any selection, you may return the books for an immediate refund!

Imagine. . .four new romances every four weeks—two historical, two contemporary—with men and women like you who long to meet the one God has chosen as the love of their lives. . .all for the low price of $9.97 postpaid.

*To join, simply complete the coupon below and mail to the address provided.* **Heartsong Presents** romances are rated G for another reason: They'll arrive *Godspeed!*